TWISTED JOURNEYS® #15

Agent Mongoose and the Attack of the Giant Insects

Marie P. Croall & Dan Jolley

illustrated by Matt Wendt

GRAPHIC UNIVERSE™ · MINNEAPOLIS · NEW YORK

Story by Marie P. Croall and Dan Jolley

Pencils and inks by Matt Wendt

Coloring by Hi-Fi Design

Lettering by Marshall Dillon

Graphic Universe
A division of Lerner Publishing Group, Inc.
241 First Avenue North
Minneapolis, MN 55401 U.S.A.

Website address: www.lernerbooks.com

Library of Congress Cataloging-in-Publication Data

Croall, Marie P.
        Agent Mongoose and the attack of the giant insects / by Marie P. Croall & Dan Jolley ; illustrated by Matt Wendt.
             p.   cm. — (Twisted journeys ; [#15])
        Summary: As the youngest operative in a secret agency, the reader is asked to make choices throughout the story to save the world from an invasion of monstrous bugs.
        ISBN: 978–0–8225–9251–8 (lib. bdg. : alk. paper)
        1. Plot-your-own stories. 2. Graphic novels. [1. Graphic novels. 2. Spies—Fiction. 3. Insects—Fiction. 4. Plot-your-own stories.] I. Jolley, Dan. II. Wendt, Matt, ill. III. Title.
PZ7.7.C76At 2010
[Fic]—dc22   2009013876

Manufactured in the United States of America
1 – DP – 7/15/10

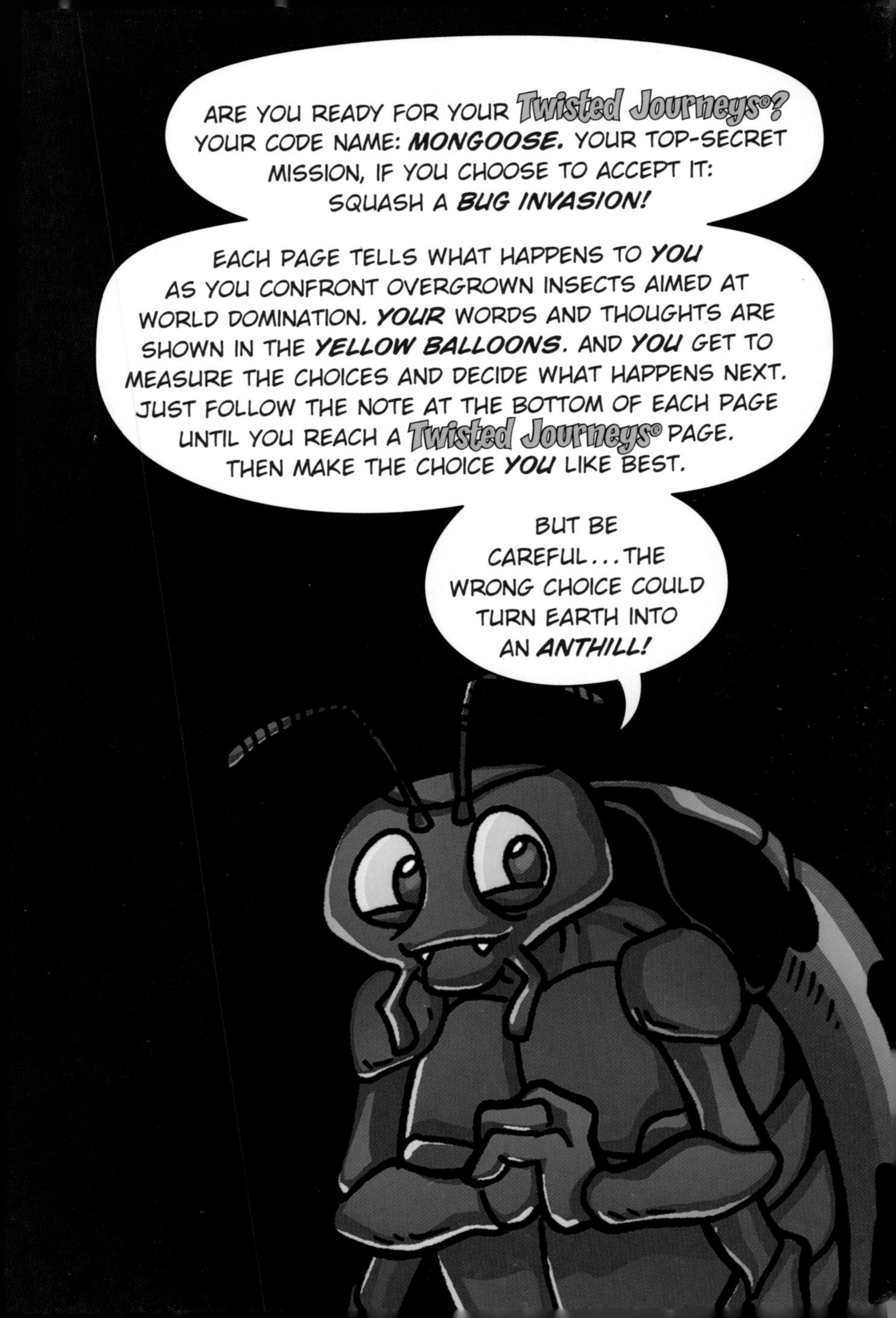
ARE YOU READY FOR YOUR Twisted Journeys®? YOUR CODE NAME: MONGOOSE. YOUR TOP-SECRET MISSION, IF YOU CHOOSE TO ACCEPT IT: SQUASH A BUG INVASION!
EACH PAGE TELLS WHAT HAPPENS TO YOU AS YOU CONFRONT OVERGROWN INSECTS AIMED AT WORLD DOMINATION. YOUR WORDS AND THOUGHTS ARE SHOWN IN THE YELLOW BALLOONS. AND YOU GET TO MEASURE THE CHOICES AND DECIDE WHAT HAPPENS NEXT. JUST FOLLOW THE NOTE AT THE BOTTOM OF EACH PAGE UNTIL YOU REACH A Twisted Journeys® PAGE. THEN MAKE THE CHOICE YOU LIKE BEST.
BUT BE CAREFUL . . . THE WRONG CHOICE COULD TURN EARTH INTO AN ANTHILL!

"You're clear to go, Mongoose," Miss Worthington's voice whispers through your earpiece.

You look around the enormous warehouse. Stacks of huge crates obstruct your view. Anything could be lurking out there in the darkness. You power up your SINDR (Subatomic Interference/Neural Disruptor Ray) and creep silently out from the shadows.

Suddenly you hear the roar of an engine, and a pile of crates bursts apart in a fiery explosion. Metal treads clank across the concrete floor as an enormous tank rolls into view. The cannon swivels, zeroing in on you.

You recognize the model. It's a Chekov 117—and the 117 has a weak spot where the turret joins the body. Before the tank has a chance to fire again, you roll to the side and trigger your SINDR. Electricity crackles along an ionized stream of air and connects with the tank . . .

. . . and the huge vehicle shuts down.

You've done it again: you've saved the free world.

"Good work, Mongoose," Miss Worthington's voice crackles in your ear. "Now get back to headquarters. We've got a major situation developing."

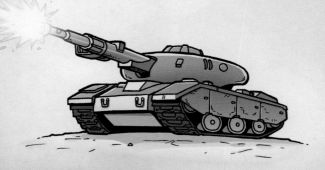

4

GO ON TO THE NEXT PAGE.

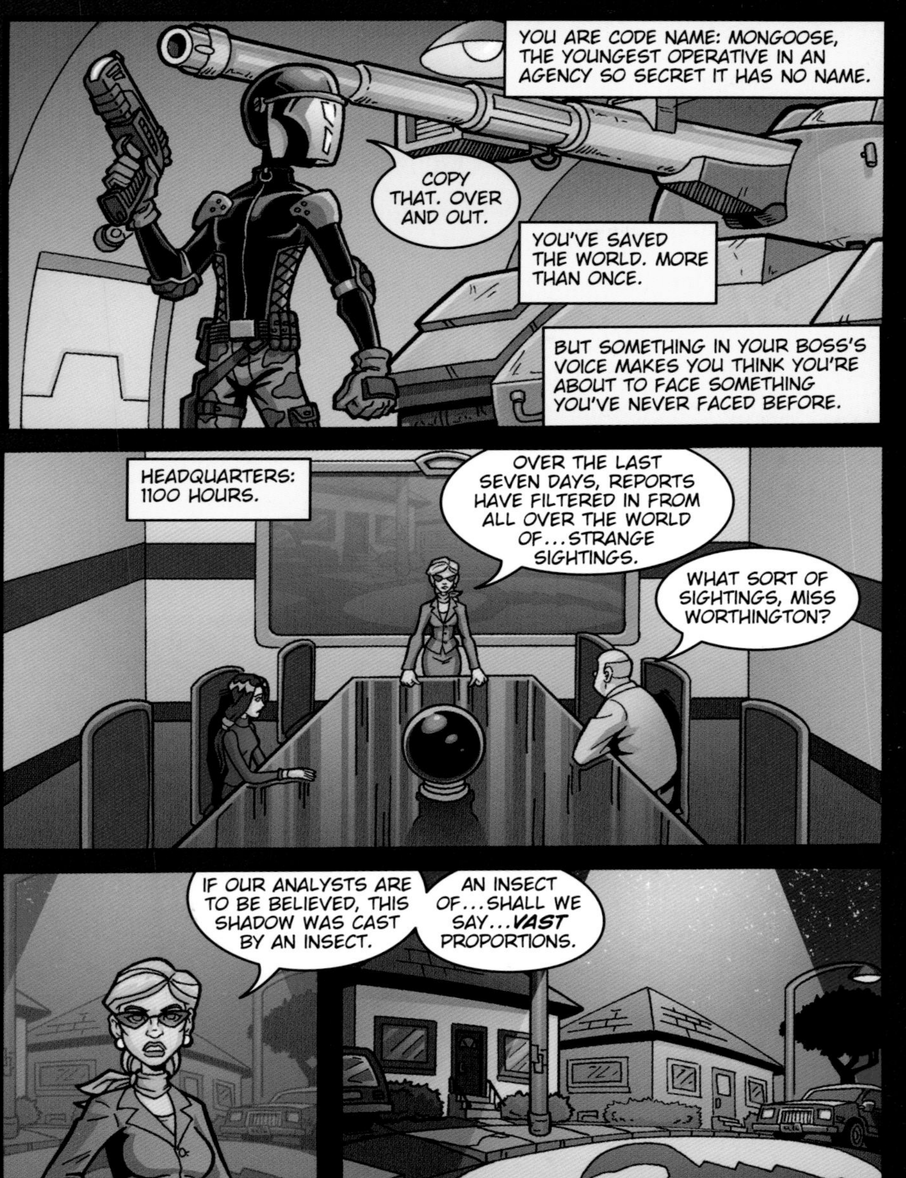
YOU ARE CODE NAME: MONGOOSE, THE YOUNGEST OPERATIVE IN AN AGENCY SO SECRET IT HAS NO NAME.
COPY THAT. OVER AND OUT.
YOU'VE SAVED THE WORLD. MORE THAN ONCE.
BUT SOMETHING IN YOUR BOSS'S VOICE MAKES YOU THINK YOU'RE ABOUT TO FACE SOMETHING YOU'VE NEVER FACED BEFORE.
HEADQUARTERS: 1100 HOURS.
OVER THE LAST SEVEN DAYS, REPORTS HAVE FILTERED IN FROM ALL OVER THE WORLD OF...STRANGE SIGHTINGS.
WHAT SORT OF SIGHTINGS, MISS WORTHINGTON?
IF OUR ANALYSTS ARE TO BE BELIEVED, THIS SHADOW WAS CAST BY AN INSECT.
AN INSECT OF...SHALL WE SAY...*VAST* PROPORTIONS.

GO ON TO THE NEXT PAGE.

"We need to find out what it is and take care of it." Miss Worthington looks around the table. "Agent Vermilion, you'll be on information control. Make sure no further word of this gets out to the press. We don't need a panic on our hands."

Vermilion nods. "Not a problem."

"Agent Snowbank, you're on analysis. Offer any assistance possible to our researchers."

"Of course," Snowbank says. "Whatever evidence we've got, we'll get the most out of it."

That leaves you! Miss Worthington pushes a manila folder across the table toward you. "You're on location and containment, Mongoose. Your previous fieldwork leads me to believe you're the best agent for the job. Don't prove me wrong."

You flip through the file, which details all the locations of the strange sightings. "Where do you want me to start?"

"You can try to use the lab's remote locators, or you can head out to the most recent sighting. Your choice."

TWISTED JOURNEYS®

What'll it be?

WILL YOU . . .

. . . try to track these "giant insects"
remotely, from the agency lab?
TURN TO PAGE 18.

. . . head out into the field?
TURN TO PAGE 82.

NEW YORK. CHICAGO. LOS ANGELES. WE HAVE ENOUGH EGGS FOR ONE MORE.

PERHAPS CLEVELAND...?

YOU'RE NOT SENDING THOSE EGGS *ANYWHERE*, RAZONOFF!

WHO ARE YOU PEOPLE? WHAT DO YOU THINK YOU'RE DOING?

YOU DON'T NEED TO KNOW OUR NAMES.

JUST KNOW: THIS *BOMB* AND I ARE TELLING YOU TO SHUT THIS WHOLE OPERATION DOWN. RIGHT *NOW*.

HMMM. WELL I THINK...

...THAT YOU ARE *BLUFFING.* BOYS, TAKE THIS GARBAGE OUT.

HEY, *WAIT* A SECOND--!

PLASTIC EXPLOSIVE BOMBS ARE PRETTY DEPENDABLE. THEY DON'T TEND TO JUST GO OFF BY THEMSELVES, LIKE TOO-OLD DYNAMITE SOMETIMES DOES.

BUT WHEN A RANDOM *FINGER* HITS THE *TRIGGER* BUTTON...

THAT MEANS IT'S...

THE END

You and Highbrow start down the middle tunnel. It twists and turns . . .

. . . and when you come around a corner, you see a dozen fat, white grubs on the ground, each one the size of a football. They're the source of the noise! To your surprise, you can't help but think of them as kind of *cute*.

But while you and Highbrow are distracted, something else has arrived. A huge mandible nudges you in the back . . .

. . . and you turn to see two enormous, mutated *cockroaches* right behind you. More of them scuttle out of the darkness ahead. You're surrounded! They scoot you toward the larvae and, to your astonishment, make you sit down with the grubs.

"This means they're adopting us," Highbrow whispers. He gives the huge insects a terrified grin. "They're making us join their colony!"

There are too many to fight past. You just hope someone *finds* you down here.

Soon . . . !

THE END

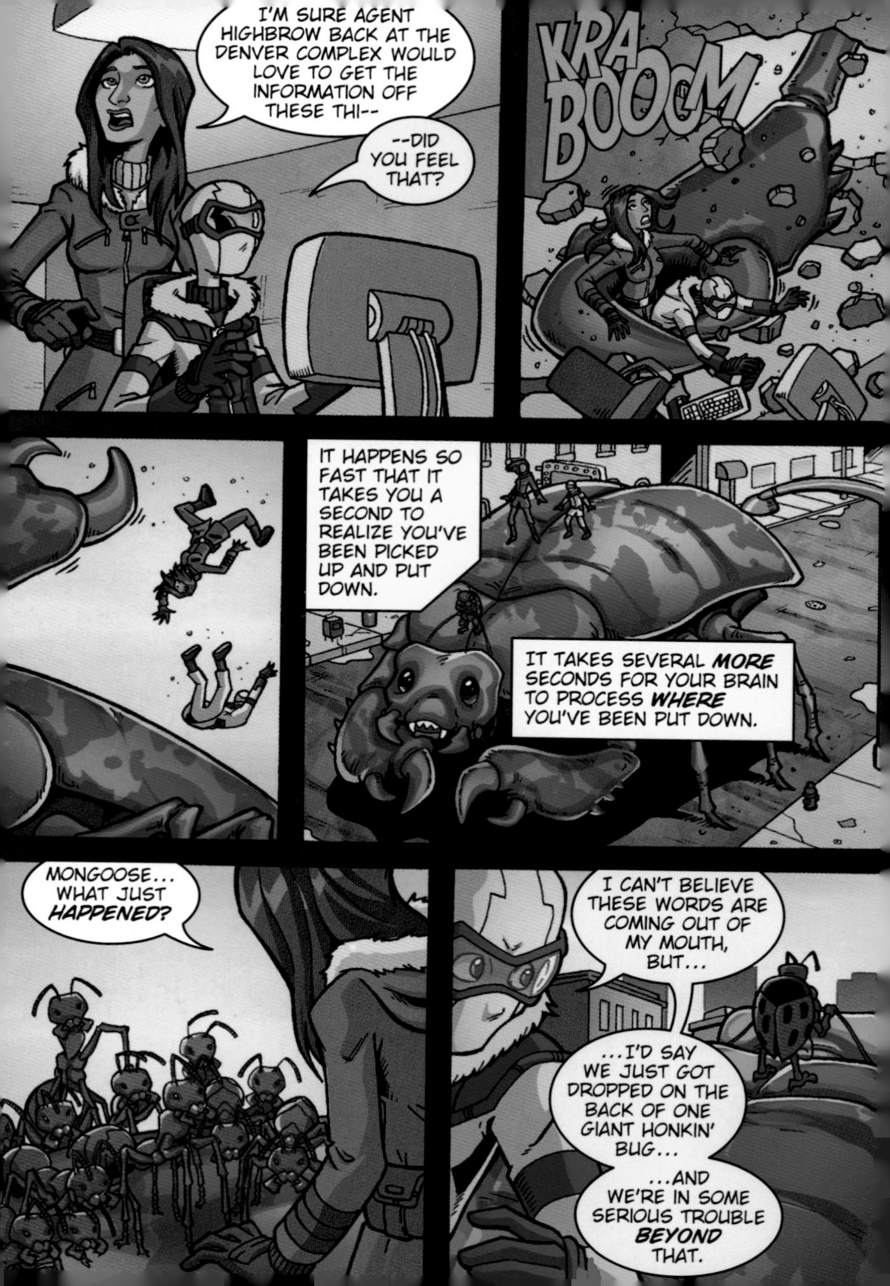
I'M SURE AGENT HIGHBROW BACK AT THE DENVER COMPLEX WOULD LOVE TO GET THE INFORMATION OFF THESE THI--
--DID YOU FEEL THAT?
KRA BOOOM
IT HAPPENS SO FAST THAT IT TAKES YOU A SECOND TO REALIZE YOU'VE BEEN PICKED UP AND PUT DOWN.
IT TAKES SEVERAL MORE SECONDS FOR YOUR BRAIN TO PROCESS WHERE YOU'VE BEEN PUT DOWN.
MONGOOSE... WHAT JUST HAPPENED?
I CAN'T BELIEVE THESE WORDS ARE COMING OUT OF MY MOUTH, BUT...
...I'D SAY WE JUST GOT DROPPED ON THE BACK OF ONE GIANT HONKIN' BUG...
...AND WE'RE IN SOME SERIOUS TROUBLE BEYOND THAT.

Neutralizing General Razonoff would be a lot easier here, with only a couple of guards, rather than dealing with all those soldiers in the room with the giant eggs. You take a deep breath . . .

. . . and kick the vent cover off, bursting out into the room.

"Alert!" Razonoff barks. "Eliminate the intruder!"

That's easier said than done, though, as you draw your ion-stream SINDR and fire point-blank at first one guard and then the other. They both fall to the floor in twitching heaps—

—but then something that feels like a baseball bat crashes into the back of your head, and you crumple to your knees.

There were two other guards in the room who you couldn't see from the ventilation shaft!

"What is this?" Razonoff laughs. "A *child*? Sent after *me*? Ridiculous. Guards. Restrain the spy. . . I'll enjoy feeding this little intruder to the ants."

THE END

In the eerie light of the transportal, you and Topaz prepare to make your move.

"Standard subdual measures?" you whisper to Topaz.

"Of course," she whispers back. "SINDRs and right crosses, not blades or bullets."

The guards don't have time to react before you reach the first one. You're impressed with Topaz's martial-arts skills, as she zaps one guard with her SINDR and knocks another one senseless with a roundhouse kick. She's almost as good as you are.

Once the guards are down and bound with zip ties, you and Topaz approach the transportal. Something about the strange device makes the hairs on the back of your neck stand up.

"So we're in agreement?" Topaz asks. "We're going to blow this thing to bits, right?"

You nod slowly. "I've never seen tech like this before, though. Almost a shame to destroy it . . . Almost."

You know this stuff has to go.
But the question is, exactly *how*?

WILL YOU . . .

. . . destroy the whole room, equipment and all?
TURN TO PAGE 26.

. . . blow up just the gate itself?
TURN TO PAGE 74.

. . . download any information you can find
before you do anything else?
TURN TO PAGE 10.

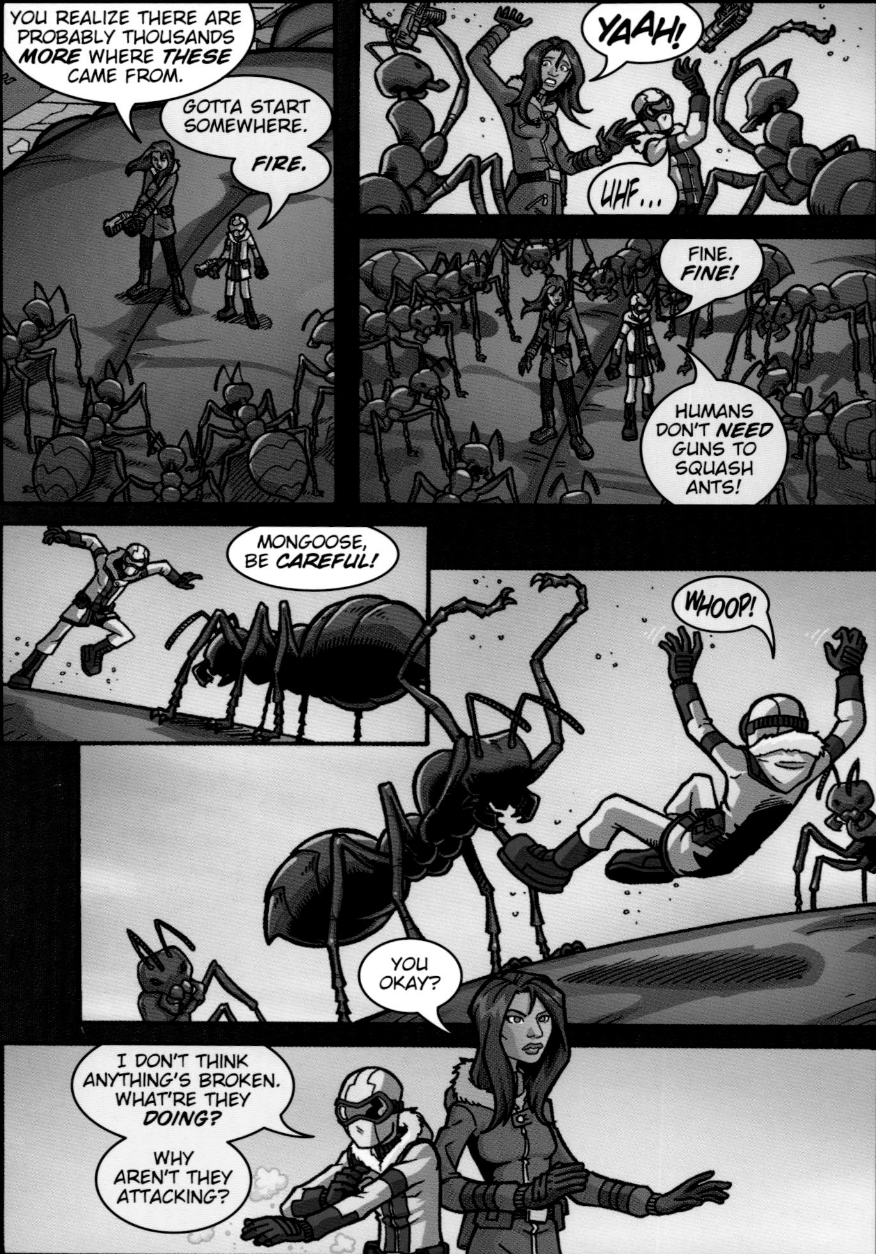
YOU REALIZE THERE ARE PROBABLY THOUSANDS MORE WHERE THESE CAME FROM.
GOTTA START SOMEWHERE.
FIRE.
YAAH!
UHF...
FINE. FINE!
HUMANS DON'T NEED GUNS TO SQUASH ANTS!
MONGOOSE, BE CAREFUL!
WHOOP!
YOU OKAY?
I DON'T THINK ANYTHING'S BROKEN. WHAT'RE THEY DOING?
WHY AREN'T THEY ATTACKING?

GO ON TO THE NEXT PAGE.

"And—wait just a minute here," you say, puzzled, looking Topaz in the eye. "Did that thing just use *judo* on me?"

One of the ants rears back onto its four hind legs—and reveals a small pouch on a harness slung across its underside. It reaches into the pouch, pulls out a small headset, and throws it to you. Slowly you put it on . . .

. . . and it's as if someone's hit a giant "MUTE" button on the world, restoring its normal volume. The insects are chatting among themselves, and they're all talking about you and Topaz!

"First human I've seen all day," one says, while another murmurs, "Wish I could have hair. I bet having hair would be fun," and a third observes, "That young child recovered better than any adult human I've ever seen!"

You turn to Topaz. "I think they're friendly!"

One of them throws her a headset too.

GO ON TO THE NEXT PAGE.

"So . . . you guys can understand me?"

One of the ants approaches you and thrusts out one hooked leg. "Sure can! The name's Roger. Roger Bumppo."

"Uh . . . why do you have a human name?" Topaz asks as you shake Roger's hand.

"We thought it'd make the process easier," Roger says.

"What process?" you ask uneasily.

"Why, annexing Planet Earth!" Roger replies, his voice cheerful. "I know we just got here and all, but well, we outnumber you by about, um . . . ten million to one, so there's not much point in resisting."

"What?! You can't just *take over* like this!"

"Sure we can!" Roger says. "Don't worry, you can all work for us! We've got a great health plan, *tons* of benefits. Would you like a company car? A corner office? We can arrange that. Come, walk with me, talk with me."

Bugs for bosses. Great.

Although . . . your own office *would* be pretty cool . . .

THE END

You've seen some strange things before. You've even seen a teleporter a time or two. But you've never seen one like *this*.

WILL YOU . . .

. . . try to find out as much about it as you can?
TURN TO PAGE 93.

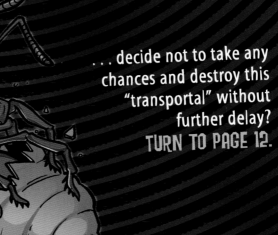

. . . decide not to take any chances and destroy this "transportal" without further delay?
TURN TO PAGE 12.

You head down to the lab. Something about this case makes you think it'll be smarter to start there.

The lab is dark—even a little creepy—and lit only by computer monitors. At first you think no one's there, but then a computer tech pops up from behind a screen and grins at you. His security badge reads Code name: Highbrow. "Hello, Mongoose! Didn't expect to see you down here!"

"What do you have for me on these possible 'giant insects?'" you ask.

"That's what I like about you, Mongoose," Agent Highbrow says. "Most of the other field agents just charge ahead. You're smarter than that. You take time for research."

"Thanks." You try not to sound impatient. "So—insects? Giant ones?"

Highbrow beckons you around, pointing at his monitor. "I just found something! C'mon, you can take a look at this with me."

GO ON TO THE NEXT PAGE.

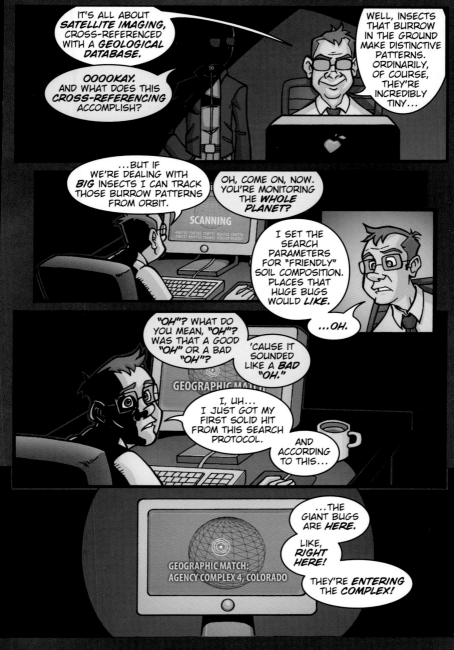

IT'S ALL ABOUT *SATELLITE IMAGING*, CROSS-REFERENCED WITH A *GEOLOGICAL DATABASE.*

OOOOKAY. AND WHAT DOES THIS *CROSS-REFERENCING* ACCOMPLISH?

WELL, INSECTS THAT BURROW IN THE GROUND MAKE DISTINCTIVE PATTERNS. ORDINARILY, OF COURSE, THEY'RE INCREDIBLY TINY...

...BUT IF WE'RE DEALING WITH *BIG* INSECTS I CAN TRACK THOSE BURROW PATTERNS FROM ORBIT.

OH, COME ON, NOW. YOU'RE MONITORING THE *WHOLE PLANET?*

I SET THE SEARCH PARAMETERS FOR "FRIENDLY" SOIL COMPOSITION. PLACES THAT HUGE BUGS WOULD *LIKE.*

...OH.

"OH"? WHAT DO YOU MEAN, *"OH"*? WAS THAT A GOOD *"OH"* OR A BAD *"OH"*?

'CAUSE IT SOUNDED LIKE A *BAD "OH."*

I, UH... I JUST GOT MY FIRST SOLID HIT FROM THIS SEARCH PROTOCOL.

AND ACCORDING TO THIS...

...THE GIANT BUGS ARE *HERE.*

LIKE, *RIGHT HERE!*

THEY'RE *ENTERING* THE *COMPLEX!*

GEOGRAPHIC MATCH: AGENCY COMPLEX 4, COLORADO

GO ON TO THE NEXT PAGE.

Something feels weird about this. If the bugs were digging into the complex, shouldn't they be attacking already?

WILL YOU . . .

. . . start searching the complex immediately?
TURN TO PAGE 42.

. . . keep using the lab equipment to investigate further?
TURN TO PAGE 58.

The three of you take the nearest staircase that isn't caved in. You don't even consider trying to find an elevator. You know that if there's any kind of emergency like a fire or an earthquake, the last place you want to be is in an elevator.

"How are we supposed to find a way out?" Topaz asks, as she takes the stairs two at a time.

"Maybe a ventilation shaft?" You look at Sikorsky expectantly.

"How should I know?" he says. "I just deal with weird animals!"

The stairs shake—and the mantis explodes through the doors below you! The monster can barely fit into the stairwell, but it claws and pushes its way up toward you . . .

. . . and you discover the door at the top is locked. There's no time to try to get it open . . .

. . . and the mantis lunges for you, its mouth gaping wide.

THE END

WELL. I'D SAY RELEASING THE GIANT BUG-EATING BUGS SOUNDS PRETTY GOOD.

WOW! **LOOK** AT ALL OF THEM!

THEY, UH, THEY WON'T **HURT** ME, WILL THEY?

THESE HAVE BEEN THE LEAST HOSTILE OF ANY OF THE GIANT INSECTS.

LEAST HOSTILE? **LEAST** HOSTILE? SO THAT MEANS **SOME** HOSTILE?

I'D TAKE **"SOME HOSTILE"** OVER **"DEFINITELY GOING TO EAT MY FACE."**

WELL, YOU'VE GOT A POINT THERE.

GUESS I'LL DO THE HONORS

BREET

K-CHAK CHANK

BZZZZ

ZZZ

ZZ

ZZ

ZZ

ZZ

ZZ

GO ON TO THE NEXT PAGE.

"Time to make a break for it," you tell Highbrow and the scientists, "while the ants are distracted."

The five of you rush through the door into the hallway and sprint toward the far end. You run through a scene of utter chaos. The ant lions attack the ants in a frenzy, but the ants swarm out of their tunnel by the hundreds . . . maybe the thousands!

Suddenly your foot hits a patch of ant juice and slips—and you find yourself tumbling headlong into a mass of ants. You fight your way out of it as fast as you can, but now the scientists have made it to safety . . . and you're on the wrong side of a huge mass of ants, cutting you off.

Then . . . from behind you . . . you hear a low, ominous whir. You turn . . .

. . . and see the giant wasp approaching, attracted by all the noise.

It looks as if your group stands a good chance of escaping! But these are *not* field agents. Most of them couldn't even run a red light.

WILL YOU . . .

. . . catch up with the group and try to make it out together? TURN TO PAGE 46.

. . . attempt to buy the group some time by facing the wasp alone? TURN TO PAGE 66.

"We can't stay here," you whisper to Topaz. "There are too many of them. We have to do something else."

"But the explosives! We need to take these bugs out!"

"The bombs won't do any good if we can't get them set. Come on."

You turn to start heading back out of the tunnel—and that's when you realize that two of the mantises have been sneaking up right behind you, ready to strike. You should have realized: this is how praying mantises hunt! They were hiding in alcoves in the tunnel that you didn't even see when you were approaching the chamber. And now that you're within range, you know they'll strike with blinding speed.

"Look out!" you scream and shove Topaz out of the way, just as a gigantic claw slashes through the air where she was standing.

But when the other mantis attacks, you're not as lucky.

THE END

YOU'RE TAKING NO CHANCES ON ANY OF THIS. IT'S **ALL** GOING AWAY.

THE COAST STILL CLEAR, TOPAZ?

YEAH, TOTALLY QUIET. I THINK WE'RE ALONE--

--IN HERE.

GOOD EVENING, LITTLE HUMANS.

KRAKK

WELCOME...

...TO THE **LAST** DAY OF THE REST OF YOUR LIVES.

Neither you nor Topaz has any idea how to fight this creature. You know how to block punches and kicks, but only two of each. This thing has six limbs, and they all seem ready to claw and slash and bludgeon.

"You don't have a chance," the Razonoff creature snarls. "I'm going to make you both my servants. The only two humans in my insect army! Won't that be a sight to see!"

Topaz takes a breath to answer, but you never hear what she would have said . . .

. . . because at that moment, your charges start going off.

The transportal begins to topple, and as it does, a brilliant sphere of white energy flashes out of it and splashes across the floor like a glowing wave.

"What's happening?" Topaz shouts.

"I have no idea!" you answer her . . . and then you notice that you, Topaz, *and* the Razonoff creature are all *glowing*.

GO ON TO THE NEXT PAGE.

Suddenly you feel as if you're falling, even though you can still feel your feet on the floor. The world around you goes white . . . and then you start to get strange glimpses, as if you're plummeting past a series of windows. Through each window, you can see an entirely different world, but only for a split second. There's one populated by people made of rock . . . one where green snow falls in a blizzard . . . one that smells like a mixture of gasoline and peaches.

Abruptly, everything comes to a halt.

You, Topaz, and the Razonoff monster are all stuck in a colossal spiderweb, with strands as thick as your arm. The web vibrates, and a spider the size of a Winnebago scuttles over and looks down at you.

"Ah, sentient beings," the spider says, chuckling. "Usually I just have mindless bugs for dinner. This will be a treat."

THE END

The agency never trained you for *this!*

WILL YOU . . .

. . . fight the big hairy ants?
TURN TO PAGE 14.

. . . try to escape by climbing down the huge beetle's leg?
TURN TO PAGE 104.

. . . approach the "driver" at the huge beetle's head?
TURN TO PAGE 78.

The bombs can wait! You drop the transmitter and shout, "Behind you!"

Topaz whirls and ducks out of the way . . . but your raised voice suddenly gets the attention of every huge insect in the chamber.

You and Topaz back away from the one that almost tagged her. "Arm the bombs!" she hisses. "You've got to arm the bombs before these things can escape!"

You know she's right—but the transmitter's on the ground, and you see that a dozen huge mantises are blocking your way to it. In fact, glancing around the chamber, you see that the mantises have you and Topaz surrounded.

"I don't think we're getting out of here," Topaz says, her voice flat and hopeless.

"Maybe not," you answer, "but we're taking these monsters with us."

You dive between two of the bugs . . .

. . . and just as an enormous mantis claw spears down toward you, you hit the transmitter button.

IN MEMORIAM:
AGENTS MONGOOSE
AND TOPAZ, BURIED IN
A TUNNEL COLLAPSE.
THEY GAVE THEIR LIVES
FOR THE FREEDOM OF
THE WORLD.

THE END

WHAT COULD BE CAUSING THAT LIGHT? I'VE NEVER SEEN ANYTHING LIKE IT.

I DON'T KNOW. IT'S TOO BRIGHT FOR *CAVE FUNGUS*, THAT'S FOR SURE.

WELL *THERE'S* SOMETHING YOU DON'T SEE EVERY DAY.

YOU DO IF YOU WATCH A LOT OF SCIENCE FICTION.

HOLY *COW!* LOOK AT THAT!

IT'S LIKE THIS PORTAL IS *GRABBING* THESE GIANT BUGS FROM...FROM SOME *OTHER PLACE.* MAYBE SOME OTHER *WORLD.*

I'M AT A LOSS HERE, MONGOOSE. WHAT DO YOU WANT TO DO?

TURN TO PAGE 17.

You and Topaz grab Sikorsky and dash out of the lab.
You hear the glass shattering and the mantis roaring
behind you, and the floor and walls shake with the
impacts of the creature's claws.

"We've got to seal that thing in here!" you tell Sikorsky.
"We can't risk letting it get out!"

"There's an emergency lockdown switch near the main
entrance," he pants.

"Take us to it!" Topaz says, but before Sikorsky can
even point, all three of you are knocked off your feet. The
end of the hallway collapses, filling with rubble.

Sikorsky sits up, his face pale. "The mantis must have
knocked out the central support pylon! Half the structure
just collapsed! We're trapped!"

"Then how do we get out?" Topaz demands.

Sikorsky shrugs violently. "I don't know!"

"Look," you say, "we either go up
or down. There's got to be some
other way out of here."

GO ON TO THE NEXT PAGE.

Places like this aren't built with just one entrance and exit. You know there's got to be another way out.

WILL YOU . . .

. . . climb some stairs to try to get closer to the surface?

TURN TO PAGE 21.

. . . head down to try to get out through the sewer system?

TURN TO PAGE 34.

HERE! COME ON!

OH, YES, THIS *IS* QUITE PLEASANT.

ARE YOU COMPLAINING, DOC? PEOPLE WHO COMPLAIN GET TO TAKE THE *LEAD*.

I-- THAT IS--NO!

NO, NO, IT'S AS I SAID. *QUITE* PLEASANT! I MIGHT BUILD A SUMMER HOME DOWN HERE.

RUN *RUN RUN!*

BOOOM

WE'LL NEVER MAKE IT! WE'RE MANTIS FOOD!

JUST GET THROUGH THAT HATCH!

WHY? CAN IT NOT FOLLOW US?

IT'S A PRESSURE HATCH! IF I'M RIGHT...

...AND I THINK I *AM*...

...FOLLOWING US WON'T BE AN ISSUE!

JUST AS YOU WERE HOPING, THE PRESSURE HATCH MEANT THE BIG CHAMBER COULD BE *SEALED OFF*. SEALED...AND *FILLED* WITH WATER.

WELL DONE!

THANKS.

NOW YOU'LL HAVE *PLENTY* OF TIME TO FIND YOUR WAY OUT AND BRING BACK ENOUGH PEOPLE TO *DEAL* WITH THIS SITUATION.

THE END

Back in the corridor, you and Topaz confer in whispers. "If those eggs hatch, they're going to be a lot harder to contain than General Razonoff and his goons," Topaz says.

"I agree," you tell her. "I'm pretty sure I can dismantle all that egg-enlarging machinery, if we can figure out how to get clear access to it. Plus, y'know, if I can't turn it off, I can see about blowing it up."

She nods. "I like this plan. But you've got a bit more technical expertise than I do, and more to the point, you're the one with the explosives."

You can't help but agree. "How good are you with causing diversions?"

Topaz grins. "Watch and learn." She produces a device sort of like a small flare gun.

"What's that?"

She pops a little cartridge into it. "It's a flash-bang gun. Get ready to dismantle, okay?"

SOMETHING DOESN'T FEEL RIGHT ABOUT THIS.

THE PLAN *SEEMS* TO BE UNFOLDING PERFECTLY.

THE GUARDS *DO* GO RUNNING TO SEE WHAT HAPPENED.

YOU *ARE* ABLE TO ZIP INTO THE ROOM UNSEEN.

BUT YOU'VE GOT A FEELING... A FEELING THAT THINGS ARE GOING *TOO* SMOOTHLY.

SO MUCH SO THAT WHEN SOMETHING DOES GO HAYWIRE, YOU'RE NOT *THAT* SURPRISED.

36

GO ON TO THE NEXT PAGE.

You're not sure what, exactly, but *something* has gone very, very wrong with the equipment. Instead of shutting down, the radiation beams intensify . . .

. . . and abruptly one of the giant insect eggs hatches. Then another . . . and another! Before you know it, every egg in every cage bursts open.

That gets the guards' attention. General Razonoff runs back into the room, staring in horror at the huge number of newly hatched ants swarming out of the eggs.

And each one of those "baby" ants is the size of a kitten.

"Get out of there!" Topaz calls to you from the corridor, but it's too late: before you can even move, the ants cut off one side of the room and the guards come pouring in from the other.

Whether it'll be because of guards' bullets or giant ants' mandibles, you know that this mission has come to a messy close.

THE END

That is one big, weird, ugly bug—
but what if it's friendly?

WILL YOU . . .

. . . stop Topaz from SINDRing it?
TURN TO PAGE 52.

. . . go ahead and let Topaz fire away—even
though that *might* kill the thing?
TURN TO PAGE 91.

. . . try to just knock it out yourself?
TURN TO PAGE 77.

"If we follow those voices, maybe we can figure out who's behind this," you tell Topaz. She agrees.

The tunnel soon emerges through a hole in a cinder block wall into another part of the prison. You're in a long corridor, and light spills out into it through a doorway just ahead.

Motioning for Topaz to follow, you peek through the door.

Your breath catches in your throat. Armed military guards stand around a huge number of cages filled with what appear to be giant insect eggs. Each cage is connected to a bank of machinery that seems to be bathing it in some sort of radiation. As you watch, you see some of the eggs get *bigger*. In the middle of the room is a man you recognize: former Russian army general Sergei Razonoff.

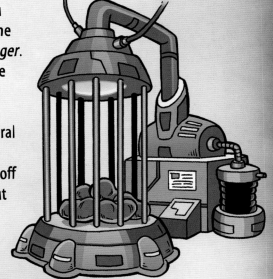

You knew Razonoff was dangerous. But crazy? Would he really breed giant bugs?

GO ON TO THE NEXT PAGE.

You've got the guy responsible for this whole mess right in front of you . . . but you've also got a boatload of giant bug eggs that could hatch at any second.

WILL YOU . . .

. . . try to destroy the eggs first?
TURN TO PAGE 35.

. . . go after General Razonoff?
TURN TO PAGE 54.

"You want me, you mutant weirdo? You'll have to catch me!" With those words, you take off as fast as you can back down the hallway, away from Highbrow and the other scientists.

Whether it's because of your shouted insult or—more likely—because you punched it in the face, the wasp comes after you with no further urging.

You put everything you've got into staying ahead of it. Every last ounce of energy goes to pumping your arms and legs as fast as you can. But no matter how fast you might be able to run . . .

. . . the wasp can *fly*. The terrible whir of its wings grows louder and louder, and then its legs close around your arms. The wasp lifts you off the floor, turns, and begins making its way back toward its nest.

The first sting, you discover, hurts more than the ones that follow . . .

THE END

Highbrow stabs a button on his keyboard and speaks into a small microphone. "Security breach! Level 10 security breach! Everyone on high alert!" He sits back, waiting to hear the response . . .

. . . and nothing happens. He looks up at you with wide eyes. "Communications are shut down! What do we do?"

You glance around the lab. All of a sudden, it's a whole lot creepier. "If these giant bugs are here in the compound . . . the first step is going to be finding them. Do you have something that could help with that?"

Highbrow thinks. "Well . . . insects communicate through chemicals called pheromones. And if these bugs are huge . . . they'd be putting out a *lot* of pheromones. Maybe I have something that could track intense chemical traces . . ."

He rummages through a shelf in the back of the room and comes up with a device that looks a little like an eggbeater. "Eureka!"

42

GO ON TO THE NEXT PAGE.

ALL RIGHT. IF THIS THING IS ACCURATE... HUH.

WELL, NO ONE'S BEEN BACK THERE IN MONTHS. IT GOT SHUT DOWN AFTER AN UNFORTUNATE ACCIDENT WITH WEAPONIZED SKUNK GLANDS.

GOOD. MAYBE WE WON'T HAVE TO *RESCUE* ANYONE.

I'M GETTING A READING FROM BACK IN LAMBDA SECTION.

W-W-WE? YOU WANT *ME* TO GO BACK THERE WITH YOU?

CAN YOU TEACH ME TO USE THAT PHEROMONE DETECTOR IN THE NEXT TEN SECONDS?

WELL... NO.

THEN YOU'RE COMING WITH ME.

SHOULD'VE CALLED IN SICK...

HAD A HEADACHE THIS MORNING, *COULD'VE* CALLED IN SICK...

BUT NOOO...

I'M GUESSING THIS CORRIDOR DIDN'T ALWAYS END LIKE THAT.

WOW...

THE DEATHLY SILENCE OF THE TUNNEL TO THE LEFT MAKES YOUR SKIN CRAWL. A DISTURBING CRUNCHING SOUND COMES FROM THE ONE IN THE MIDDLE...AND A BIZARRE SMELL WAFTS UP FROM THE RIGHT.

GO ON TO THE NEXT PAGE.

43

You're not thrilled about *any* of these . . . but you know you have to press forward.

WILL YOU . . .

. . . head down the deathly silent tunnel?
TURN TO PAGE 57.

. . investigate those strange sounds?
TURN TO PAGE 9.

. . follow your nose and check out that smell?
TURN TO PAGE 111.

With the wasp close on your heels, you duck through a doorway you haven't been through before . . .

. . . and find yourself in what appears to be a small chemical warehouse. Shelf after shelf line the walls, and aisles of shelves fill the room. You quickly lose yourself in the aisles. You can hear the wasp buzzing angrily as it tries to find you.

"Something . . . gotta be something here I can use," you say to yourself, rummaging through the unfamiliar chemicals. Something that can stop the wasp or at least generate a smoke screen so you can escape.

Desperation makes your hands move swiftly. You combine the ingredients of three different jars, making a foul-looking greenish gray liquid. And when the wasp comes around a corner and spots you, you smash the jar on the floor directly under it.

Unfortunately, you're no scientist, and this new chemical combination makes the wasp get *bigger* . . . and much *faster* . . .

THE END

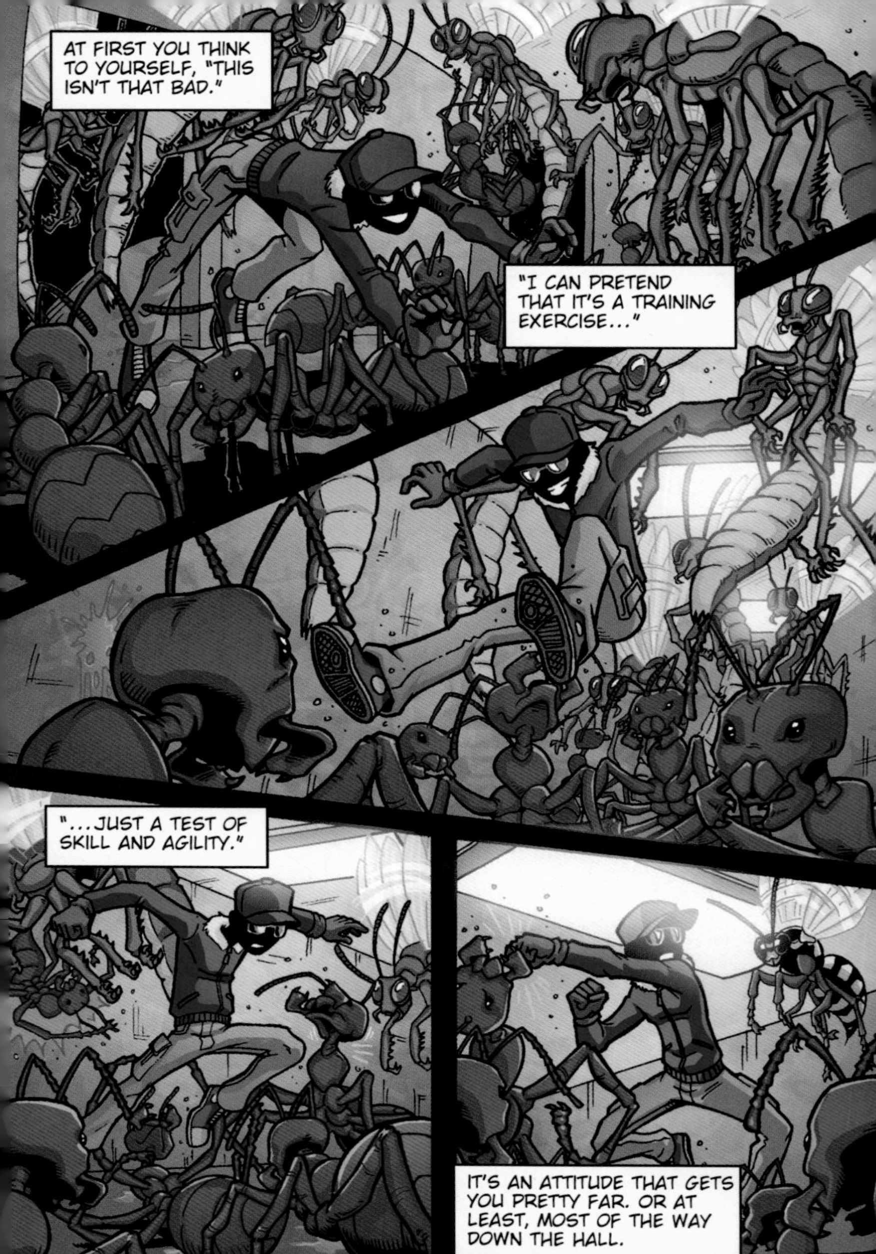
AT FIRST YOU THINK TO YOURSELF, "THIS ISN'T THAT BAD."
"I CAN PRETEND THAT IT'S A TRAINING EXERCISE..."
"...JUST A TEST OF SKILL AND AGILITY."
IT'S AN ATTITUDE THAT GETS YOU PRETTY FAR. OR AT LEAST, MOST OF THE WAY DOWN THE HALL.

You're almost there—the door is only a few feet away, with Highbrow and the scientists on the other side, cheering you on. But the wasp is following you! If you go through the door, it'll be right on your heels, and that won't accomplish anything. Out of the corner of your eye, you see an ant tunnel . . .

. . . and then you feel a tremendous impact in your side as a huge ant rams into you. You tumble down the tunnel, and the stream of ants follows you . . .

. . . as you fall into a pit at the bottom. The walls are too smooth to climb.

All the ants start flowing over the sides, dropping down to where you are.

And then the wasp descends, toward you, its wings humming.

Well . . . at least Highbrow and the white coats got out safely.

THE END

You lock eyes with Topaz. "Come on—the agency trained us to deal with crisis situations. We can take this thing down!"

Topaz gives you a tight smile and nods, and both of you draw your ion-stream SINDRs . . .

. . . just as the mantis lets out what you can only call a *roar*.

"It's getting bigger!" Sikorsky shouts, terrified.

He's right! The mantis is actually growing. It draws back one enormous claw and swings at the closest researchers.

"Fire! Fire!" Topaz yells, and both of you trigger your SINDRs.

Unfortunately, that only makes the gigantic creature angry. It swipes at you with the other claw, but you somersault out of the way. Agent Topaz isn't so lucky, and as the mantis draws the claw back toward itself, the bony tip catches her square on the shoulder and sends her spinning across the lab.

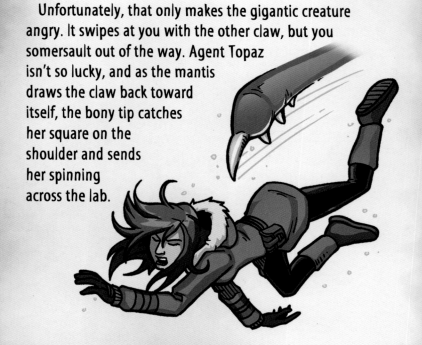

GO ON TO THE NEXT PAGE.

That was a terrible hit Topaz just took! But she's a field agent like you—you know she's tough.

WILL YOU . . .

. . . rush over and make sure she's okay?

TURN TO PAGE 69.

. . . continue fighting the mantis yourself and give her a chance to recover?

TURN TO PAGE 62.

Dividing the explosives from your pack like this will mean that each individual charge will do hardly any damage . . . but you're not going for damage. You just want noise.

While Topaz hides and waits, you set a number of charges all the way down the hall. With any luck, when you trigger the charges one at a time, more and more of the guards will come to investigate . . . and you can neutralize their threat without getting overwhelmed.

You duck into an empty closet, pull out the transmitter attuned to the bombs, and take a deep breath. "Here goes nothing," you whisper and hit the activation button.

The first charge goes off perfectly. You hear shouts and running footsteps . . . and the two guards never see you sneaking up behind them.

The second charge works just as well, as does the third . . . but then you hear Topaz shouting!

50   GO ON TO THE NEXT PAGE.

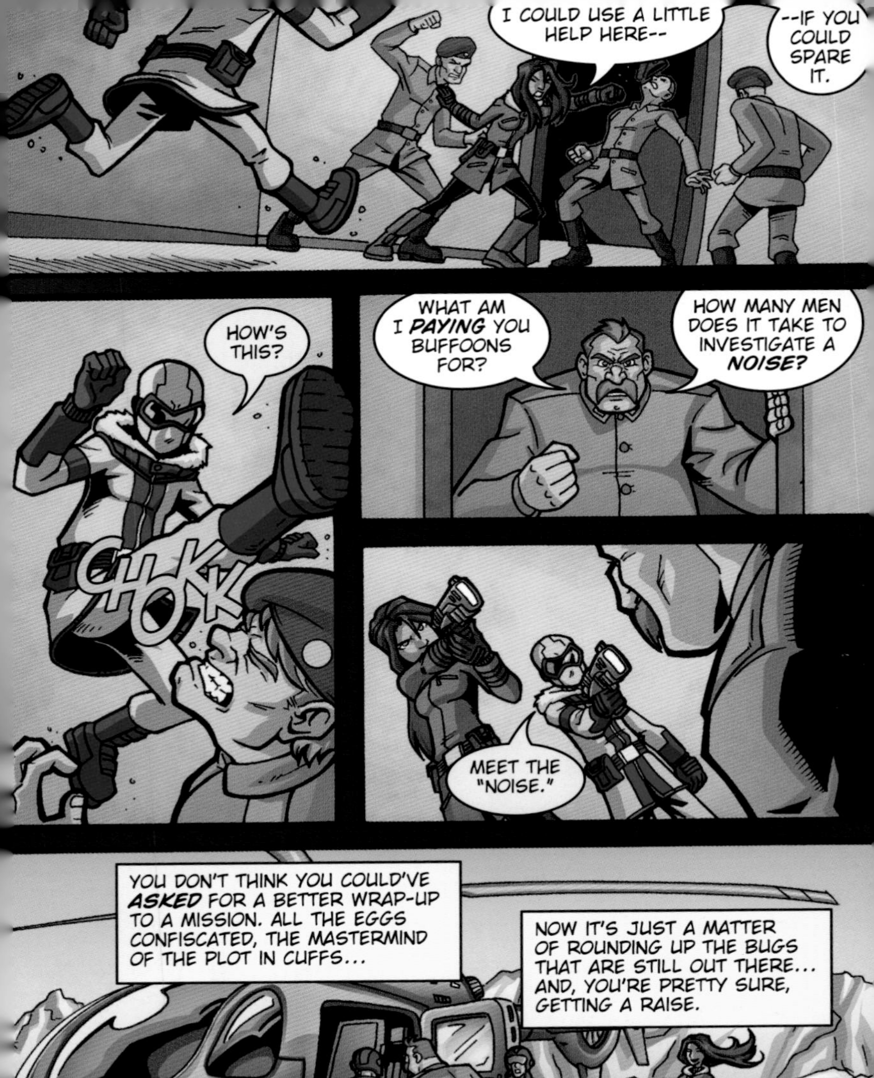
I COULD USE A LITTLE HELP HERE--
--IF YOU COULD SPARE IT.
HOW'S THIS?
CHUKKOK
WHAT AM I PAYING YOU BUFFOONS FOR?
HOW MANY MEN DOES IT TAKE TO INVESTIGATE A NOISE?
MEET THE "NOISE."
YOU DON'T THINK YOU COULD'VE ASKED FOR A BETTER WRAP-UP TO A MISSION. ALL THE EGGS CONFISCATED, THE MASTERMIND OF THE PLOT IN CUFFS...
NOW IT'S JUST A MATTER OF ROUNDING UP THE BUGS THAT ARE STILL OUT THERE... AND, YOU'RE PRETTY SURE, GETTING A RAISE.
77-E
THE END

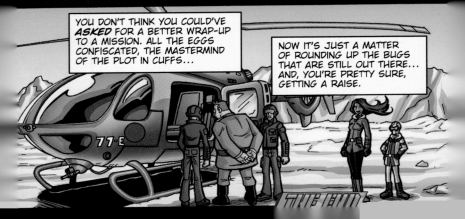

"Wait!" you shout to Topaz. She looks skeptical, but she lowers her weapon.

Quickly, you grab a set of headphones off one of the unconscious guards and put it on. Turning to the insect, you ask, "Can you understand me?"

The huge mantis looks at you with huge, sad eyes. "Where . . . is . . . family?" it asks, in a feminine voice that sounds like rustling leaves.

"Listen," you tell it, "the people who brought you here are very bad. But my friend Agent Topaz and I are going to try to help you."

The huge mantis gestures at one of the guards. "You . . . not . . . like . . . these?"

You shake your head. "No! No, they're our enemies."

Before you can do or say anything else, you hear the sound of running footsteps. More guards burst into the room behind you . . .

. . . and the mantis leaps forward, shielding you from their gunshots with its iron-hard shell.

GO ON TO THE NEXT PAGE.

Suddenly an alarm blares, and more guards rush in. "Got . . . to . . . get . . . home!" the mantis wails. "Could . . . send . . . help!" The situation is pretty desperate.

WILL YOU . . .

. . . try to reverse the transportal and let the mantis go for reinforcements?
TURN TO PAGE 70.

. . . attempt to take out the guards first?
TURN TO PAGE 65.

As you and Topaz watch, General Razonoff disappears through a door on the far wall. Topaz whispers, "Eggs never hurt anybody. I say we go after Razonoff."

"All right," you tell her, "but I want to see if there's a way to get into that back room without having to fight our way through all those guards and alert the whole complex."

She nods, and the two of you sneak past the doorway. Soon you find an empty room with a ventilation shaft opening high on the wall.

"Wait here," you say to Topaz. "I'll be right back."

She gives you a boost up. You wriggle into the ventilation shaft, moving slowly and as quietly as you can. And it's not long before you hit pay dirt: voices speaking Russian float up out of a vent cover ahead of you. You wriggle forward . . . and find yourself looking into a war room.

GO ON TO THE NEXT PAGE.

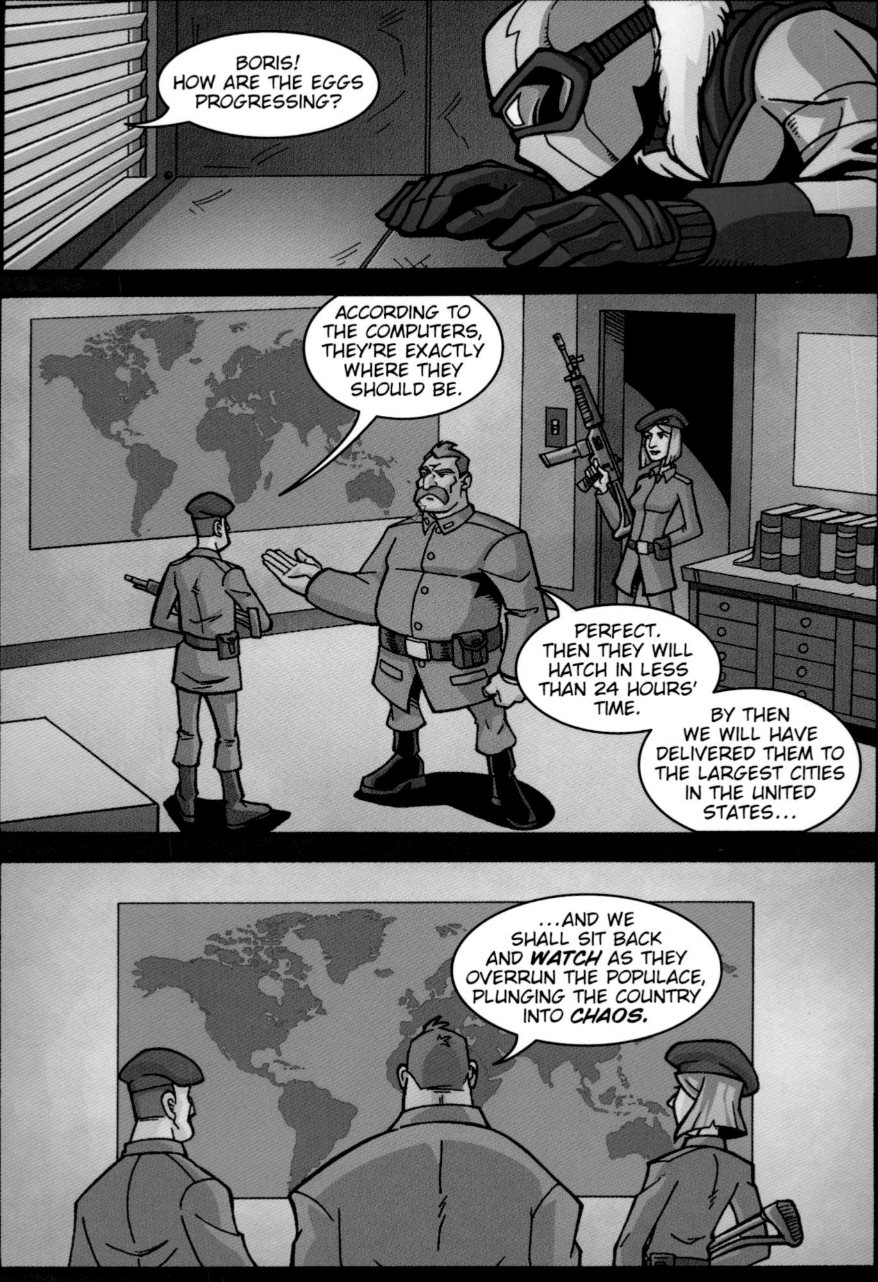
BORIS! HOW ARE THE EGGS PROGRESSING?
ACCORDING TO THE COMPUTERS, THEY'RE EXACTLY WHERE THEY SHOULD BE.
PERFECT. THEN THEY WILL HATCH IN LESS THAN 24 HOURS' TIME.
BY THEN WE WILL HAVE DELIVERED THEM TO THE LARGEST CITIES IN THE UNITED STATES...
...AND WE SHALL SIT BACK AND WATCH AS THEY OVERRUN THE POPULACE, PLUNGING THE COUNTRY INTO CHAOS.

GO ON TO THE NEXT PAGE.

TWISTED JOURNEYS®

You think you could probably act on your own
and just solve the problem right here.
But you and Topaz are a team on this . . . !

WILL YOU . . .

. . . try to neutralize General Razonoff yourself?

TURN TO PAGE 11.

. . . go back for Topaz so you
can do this together?

TURN TO PAGE 96.

Highbrow sticks close to you as you take a step through the ragged hole in the wall. The silence is so complete, it's almost deafening.

"What could've done this?" Highbrow whispers.

You examine the edges of the wall plating, and the gouges in the concrete behind it. "I don't think it was mandibles," you tell Highbrow quietly. "I'd say this looks more like . . . *claws*."

Highbrow kneels inside the tunnel, sifts through some loose dirt with one hand, and then turns and eyeballs the tunnel walls. "Oh . . . oh, no. Oh, *no*. Mongoose!"

You draw your SINDR at the panicked sound of Highbrow's voice. "*What?*"

"Whatever did this didn't tunnel *in*. It tunneled *out*! It came from inside the lab!"

That raises a ton of questions . . . but before you can ask them, a nine-foot-tall *praying mantis* appears in the tunnel behind you.

And its enormous claws lash out, *snick snack*.

THE END

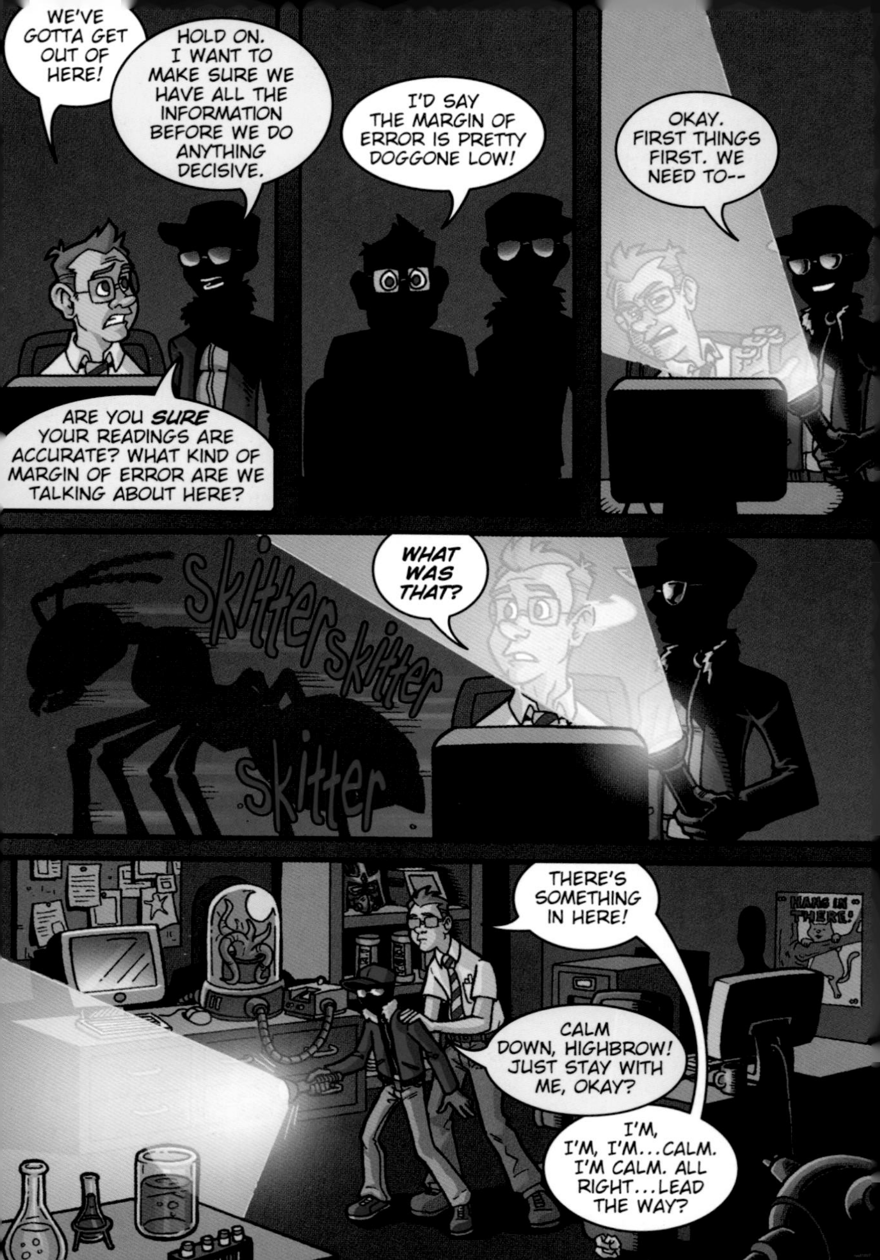

WE'VE GOTTA GET OUT OF HERE!
HOLD ON. I WANT TO MAKE SURE WE HAVE ALL THE INFORMATION BEFORE WE DO ANYTHING DECISIVE.
ARE YOU **SURE** YOUR READINGS ARE ACCURATE? WHAT KIND OF MARGIN OF ERROR ARE WE TALKING ABOUT HERE?
I'D SAY THE MARGIN OF ERROR IS PRETTY DOGGONE LOW!
OKAY. FIRST THINGS FIRST. WE NEED TO--
skitterskitter
skitter
WHAT WAS THAT?
THERE'S SOMETHING IN HERE!
CALM DOWN, HIGHBROW! JUST STAY WITH ME, OKAY?
I'M, I'M, I'M...CALM. I'M CALM. ALL RIGHT...LEAD THE WAY?
HANG IN THERE!

You and Highbrow follow the skittering sound to the back of the lab. There's a door there, concealed to look like part of the wall—but now it's standing partially open.

"What's this?" you ask, as you and Highbrow step through the door. You find yourself in a very long, dimly lit corridor lined with heavy doors.

"This is where all our genetics experiments take place," he tells you.

You stop and shine the light in Highbrow's face. "Genetic experiments? There are genetic experiments *here*? You don't think you could've *mentioned* that before now?"

"Wuh, well, it's all very—it's highly scientific, you see, and we can't—it's on a need-to-know basis. Security clearances and such."

From farther down the hallway, you hear the skittering noise again. A frown creases your brow. "Well, I hope your *security* is a big comfort when some giant bug starts gnawing on you."

GO ON TO THE NEXT PAGE.

Highbrow doesn't respond. He seems preoccupied— and he's checking out the numbers on the doors as you pass them.

"Looking for one in particular?" you ask pointedly. He glances at you and takes a breath to say something but stops himself. "You know more than you're telling me!" you hiss. "You know where these things came from, don't you?"

"It's not my department!" he wails. "I just work in computers!"

It's then that you notice the *smell*. You and Highbrow turn a corner, and you realize you're walking through a puddle of . . . "What is this?" you ask.

Highbrow aims a flashlight farther ahead and reveals the enormous body of a horse-size dead ant. "It's . . . uh . . . ant juice," he replies. Both of you reek of the stuff now.

The ant lies in a pile of rubble at the head of a tunnel torn through a wall— and right beside a ripped-open lab room.

It's impossible to tell whether the giant ant came from the tunnel or the smashed-open lab . . . or whether it's alone.

WILL YOU . . .

. . . follow the tunnel?
TURN TO PAGE 71.

. . . see what's in the laboratory?
TURN TO PAGE 98.

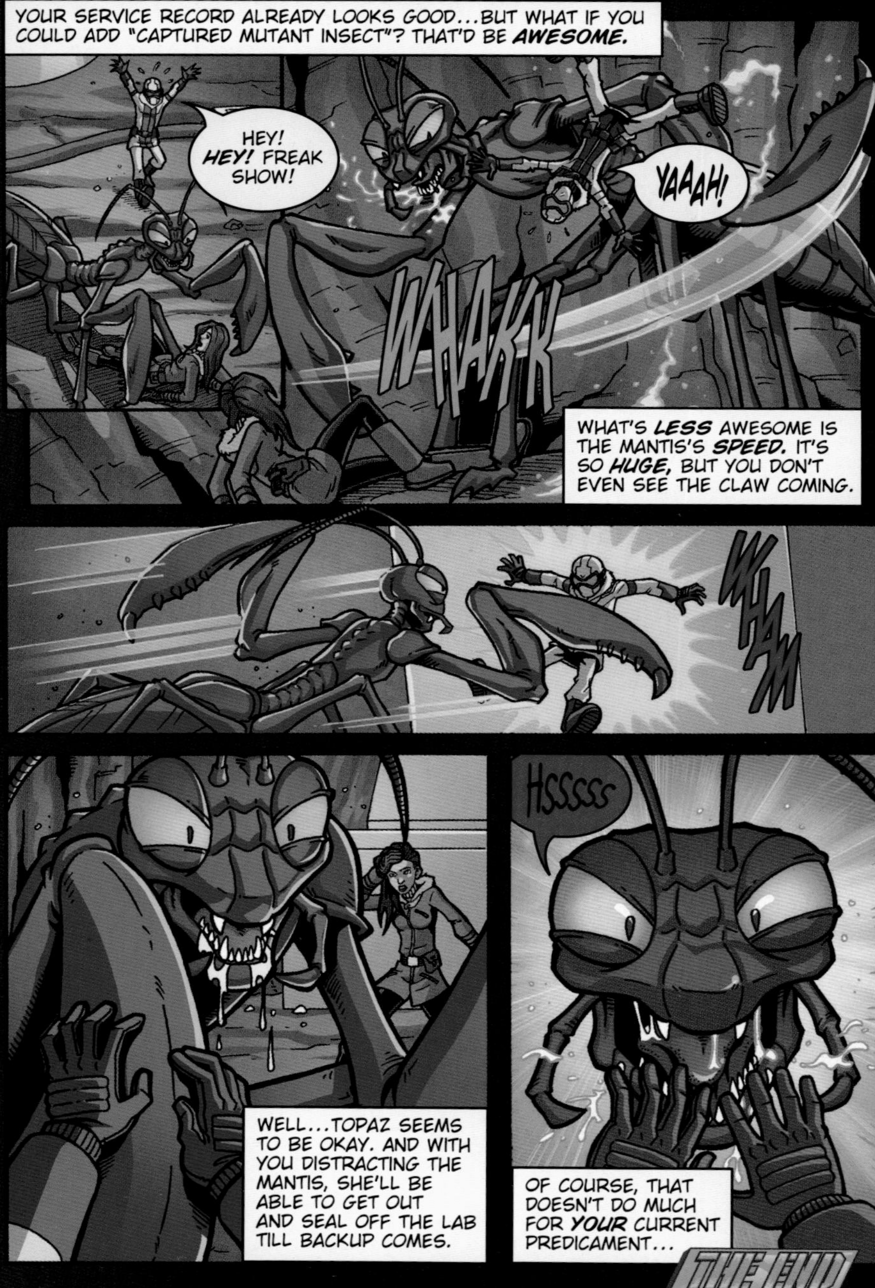
YOUR SERVICE RECORD ALREADY LOOKS GOOD...BUT WHAT IF YOU COULD ADD "CAPTURED MUTANT INSECT"? THAT'D BE ***AWESOME.***
HEY! ***HEY!*** FREAK SHOW!
YAAAH!
WHAKK
WHAT'S ***LESS*** AWESOME IS THE MANTIS'S ***SPEED.*** IT'S SO ***HUGE,*** BUT YOU DON'T EVEN SEE THE CLAW COMING.
WHAM
WELL...TOPAZ SEEMS TO BE OKAY. AND WITH YOU DISTRACTING THE MANTIS, SHE'LL BE ABLE TO GET OUT AND SEAL OFF THE LAB TILL BACKUP COMES.
Hssssss
OF COURSE, THAT DOESN'T DO MUCH FOR ***YOUR*** CURRENT PREDICAMENT...
THE END

"We're here to investigate insects, and that sounds like insects to me," you tell Topaz. "Let's head toward those crunching noises."

"Okay, but first we ought to get geared up." She produces thin jumpsuits with filter masks and goggles attached. "These are cooling suits, with carbon dioxide filters. Some insects detect their prey from CO_2 emissions and some from body heat, so depending on what kind of bug we're hunting, this might keep them from spotting us. Plus the goggles are good for night vision."

You thank her and replace your arctic gear with the new suit. The tunnel twists and turns as you follow it . . .

. . . and then the passage opens up into a huge chamber, *filled* with giant praying mantises! These things are at least as big as you are. They seem to be making a huge nest.

"This is perfect," you whisper to Topaz. "We can get rid of them all at once!"

"Oh yeah? How?"

GO ON TO THE NEXT PAGE.

If you play your cards right, you could get rid of this whole infestation in one fell swoop. If you make a mistake, though, you'll have a whole bunch of really angry bugs after you.

WILL YOU . . .

. . . try to bring down the whole room with some carefully placed explosives?
TURN TO PAGE 81.

. . . get out while you still have the chance?
TURN TO PAGE 25.

"We've got to get rid of these guys before we can do anything," you say, just as much for the mantis as for Topaz. The mantis falls in step beside you, and when you rush forward to attack General Razonoff's troops, the giant bug fights with you.

And to your relief, instead of chomping the guards' heads off, it just bonks them really hard with its huge, rocklike claws.

Soon the floor is littered with unconscious guards. The mantis turns to you. "Help . . . get . . . family . . . back . . . You'll . . . be . . . heroes . . . to . . . us . . ."

Topaz whispers to you. "You realize we have a chance here to open up diplomatic relations with an entire world of these creatures?"

You nod. "Ms. Mantis, we're going to help you. Our whole *agency* is going to help you. How'd you like to be made an honorary secret agent?"

The mantis chitters happily. "Let's . . . get . . . to . . . work . . ."

THE END

Highbrow and the white coats are on the way to safety, and the ants are no match for the ant lions. Eventually the ants will either get driven back into their tunnels or be eaten.

That just leaves the wasp.

Its wings beat the air in a terrifying frenzy, and its six-eyed head twitches back and forth between you and the retreating scientists. You've got to prevent it from going after everyone else . . .

. . . but *how*? One sting from that ice-pick-size stinger and it'll be all over for you.

You've got no choice, though. "Hey!" you shout, waving your hands. "Hey, ugly! Look at me! Look at me!"

The wasp does look at you, but only for a second. You're pretty sure it's more interested in going after the people you're trying to rescue. There are more of them, after all.

So you step forward and punch it.

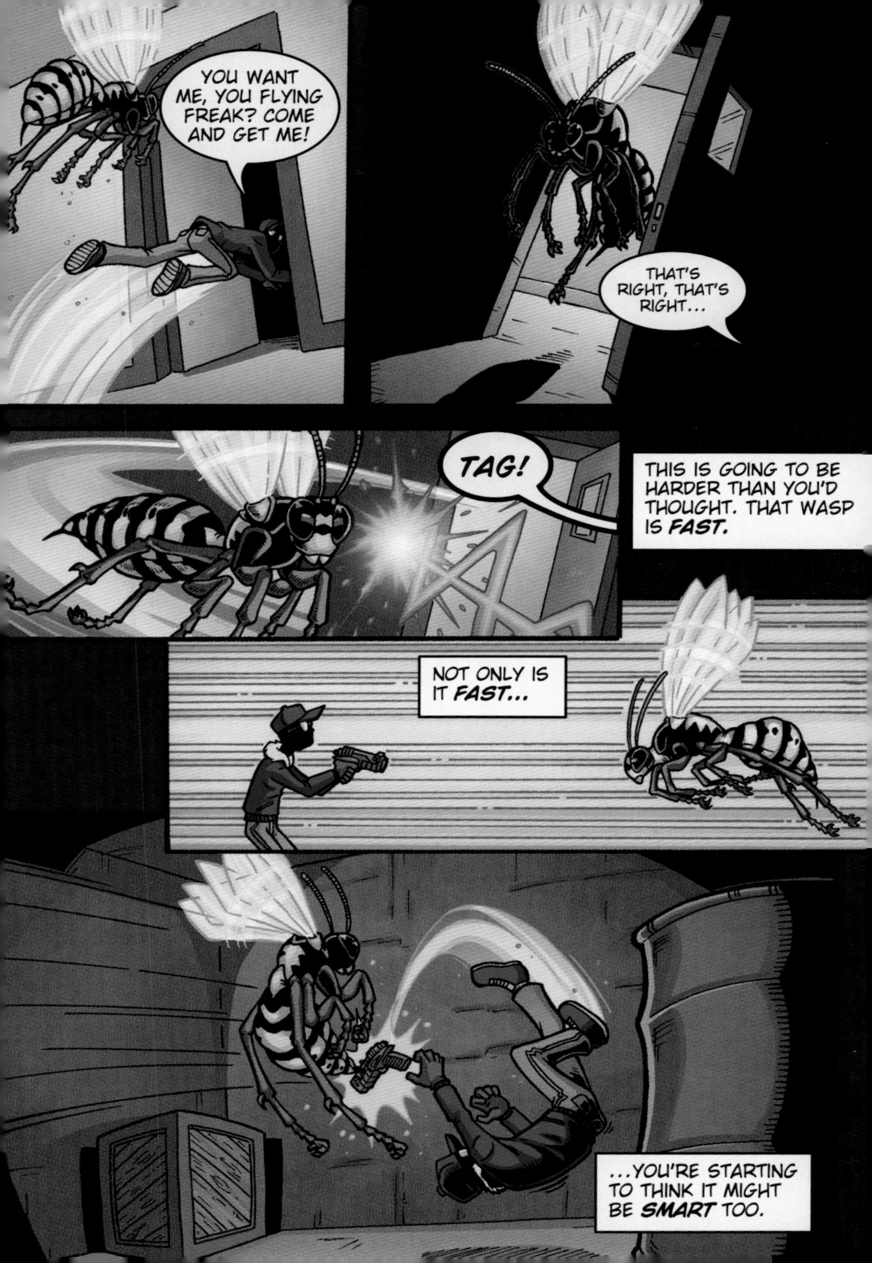
YOU WANT ME, YOU FLYING FREAK? COME AND GET ME!
THAT'S RIGHT, THAT'S RIGHT...
TAG!
THIS IS GOING TO BE HARDER THAN YOU'D THOUGHT. THAT WASP IS FAST.
NOT ONLY IS IT FAST...
...YOU'RE STARTING TO THINK IT MIGHT BE SMART TOO.

The way you see it, you've got four options.

WILL YOU . . .

. . . keep fighting the wasp and hope you get
lucky enough to disable it?
TURN TO PAGE 109.

. . . just try to escape?
TURN TO PAGE 41.

. . . look around the lab to see if you can knock the
wasp out with some sort of chemical?
TURN TO PAGE 45.

. . . try to trap the wasp in one of the big cages?
TURN TO PAGE 102.

Sikorsky has disappeared out the door, so at least you don't have to worry about him. But you have to get to Topaz and make sure she's okay!

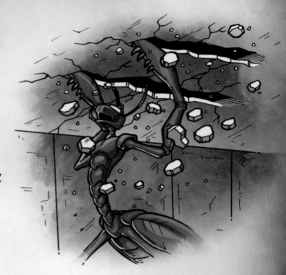

The mantis roars again and moves forward, and its footsteps make the floor shake. You jump and duck and roll across the lab, barely dodging the huge, razor-sharp claws until you make it to Topaz's side.

"Are you all right?" you ask quickly.

She groans. "I think so." Then she yells. "Look out!"

As you watch, the mantis's claws dig into the ceiling, shredding it . . . and that gives you an idea. You grab the grappling hook off Topaz's belt, fire it into the damaged ceiling, and give a huge pull . . .

. . . and the ceiling collapses on the mantis, crushing it.

You help Topaz to her feet. "Come on," you tell her. "Let's get you to a doctor. Then we'll take on the rest of the bugs together."

THE END

If the mantis can bring back help, sending her home sounds like an awfully good idea. "Cover me!" you shout to Topaz and dive toward the transportal's control panel.

"Eat hot SINDR, creeps!" Topaz screams and fires wildly into the gathering guards. You hit several buttons and flip a switch . . .

. . . and suddenly the transportal springs to life. A glowing white ball of energy pulls the mantis into it . . . and before you can react, it pulls *you* in too, with Topaz right behind you!

The two of you land on what appears to be a tree branch . . . a branch that's 30 feet wide. It's attached to a tree at least 1,000 feet tall.

And you're *surrounded* by giant praying mantises, with no transportal anywhere in sight.

The mantises all stare at you with huge eyes.

"This isn't where I wanted to spend the rest of my life," Topaz grumbles.

You can't help but agree.

THE END

THOSE LOOK LIKE THEY WERE MADE BY GIANT ANT MANDIBLES, DON'T THEY?

WELL...YEAH, I SUPPOSE SO...

THEN THAT'S WHERE WE'RE GOING.

DO YOU...*HEAR* SOMETHING?

SOMETHING THAT SOUNDS LIKE *LEGS?* *LOTS* OF LEGS?

YEEK!

GOOD CALL ON THE *LEGS* THING.

WHAT'S *THAT?*

bree-deet bree-deet

EMERGENCY SIGNAL. CARRIED BY ANOTHER FIELD AGENT.

THERE'S SOMEONE ELSE FROM THE AGENCY DOWN HERE IN THIS...COLONY.

S.O.S.

AND THE AGENT NEEDS HELP.

GO ON TO THE NEXT PAGE.

You and Agent Highbrow make your way deeper and deeper into the giant ant colony.

"Can you tell if we're getting any closer to that signal?" Highbrow asks.

"No, unfortunately. These tunnels are so confusing, I can't even tell which way is up half the time. But if there's another agent in here, we can't leave until we find him. Or her."

Highbrow coughs. You notice his eyes are watering. By way of explanation, he says, "I never knew ants smelled so *bad*."

Finally, you come to the end of a tunnel—and in the ceiling, there's a tiny opening to the outside. Directly below the opening, a large puddle of what appears to be clean, clear rainwater has collected.

"Thank goodness!" Highbrow says. "I can wash off this awful ant stink!"

You're not sure that's a good idea, though. "You *really* think this is the best time for a bath?"

GO ON TO THE NEXT PAGE.

Highbrow's right, you do both smell terrible. But do you really have the time for good grooming?

WILL YOU . . .

. . . take the opportunity to wash up in the rainwater?
TURN TO PAGE 88.

. . . just move on quickly and try to breathe through your mouth?
TURN TO PAGE 103.

"Should we be, I don't know, farther away?" Topaz asks. The two of you stand across the room from the rigged-to-explode transportal.

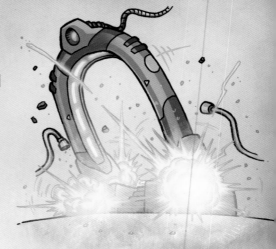

"Nah, we're safe here," you tell her. "I was very careful."

Sure enough, the charges go off, the transportal shatters . . . and both you and Topaz notice that a map of the world pops up on one of the computer monitors. "What's that for?" Topaz wonders.

And you'd answer her too, if not for the glowing white mist creeping across the floor toward you from the demolished transportal. On the world map are a number of red dots . . . destinations? Then the mist touches you . . .

. . . and, abruptly enough to make you sick to your stomach, you're *somewhere else*.

You're inside some place that used to be a building but now is like some sort of hive.

Tunnels lead off from all around you.

And you hear a lot of *skittering*.

YOU HAVE NO IDEA WHERE YOU ARE...BUT *UP* SEEMS LIKE THE RIGHT WAY TO GO, ESPECIALLY IN A PLACE LIKE THIS.

EVENTUALLY YOU AND TOPAZ DO REACH THE TOP.

AND ONCE YOU'RE THERE, YOU WISH YOU'D STAYED UNDERGROUND.

MONGOOSE, HOW...

...HOW IS THIS *POSSIBLE?*

THE EXPLANATION IS VERY SIMPLE, REALLY.

IF YOU FEEL LIKE *LISTENING.*

GO ON TO THE NEXT PAGE.

You can't tell if this thing is some sort of mutant or alien or what. You're also having a hard time deciding whether or not to run away screaming.

WILL YOU . . .

. . . talk as calmly as you can to this bizarre half bug?
TURN TO PAGE 110.

. . . decide against taking chances and just attack it?
TURN TO PAGE 95.

You step forward and, as carefully as you can, whack the bug between the eyes. The mantis slumps over, unconscious.

You and Topaz immediately go to the computer console next to the transportal and begin looking for information on the insects.

It doesn't take long before you get a sinking feeling in your stomach. "Topaz," you whisper. "According to these files, the insects are harmless! It was Razonoff controlling them—he wanted to conquer the world with a giant alien insect army!"

"That's right," Razonoff says from right behind you. You whirl around and see him kneeling next to the mantis—which is waking up.

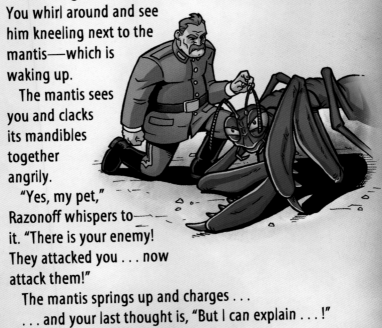

The mantis sees you and clacks its mandibles together angrily.

"Yes, my pet," Razonoff whispers to it. "There is your enemy! They attacked you . . . now attack them!"

The mantis springs up and charges . . .

. . . and your last thought is, "But I can explain . . . !"

THE END

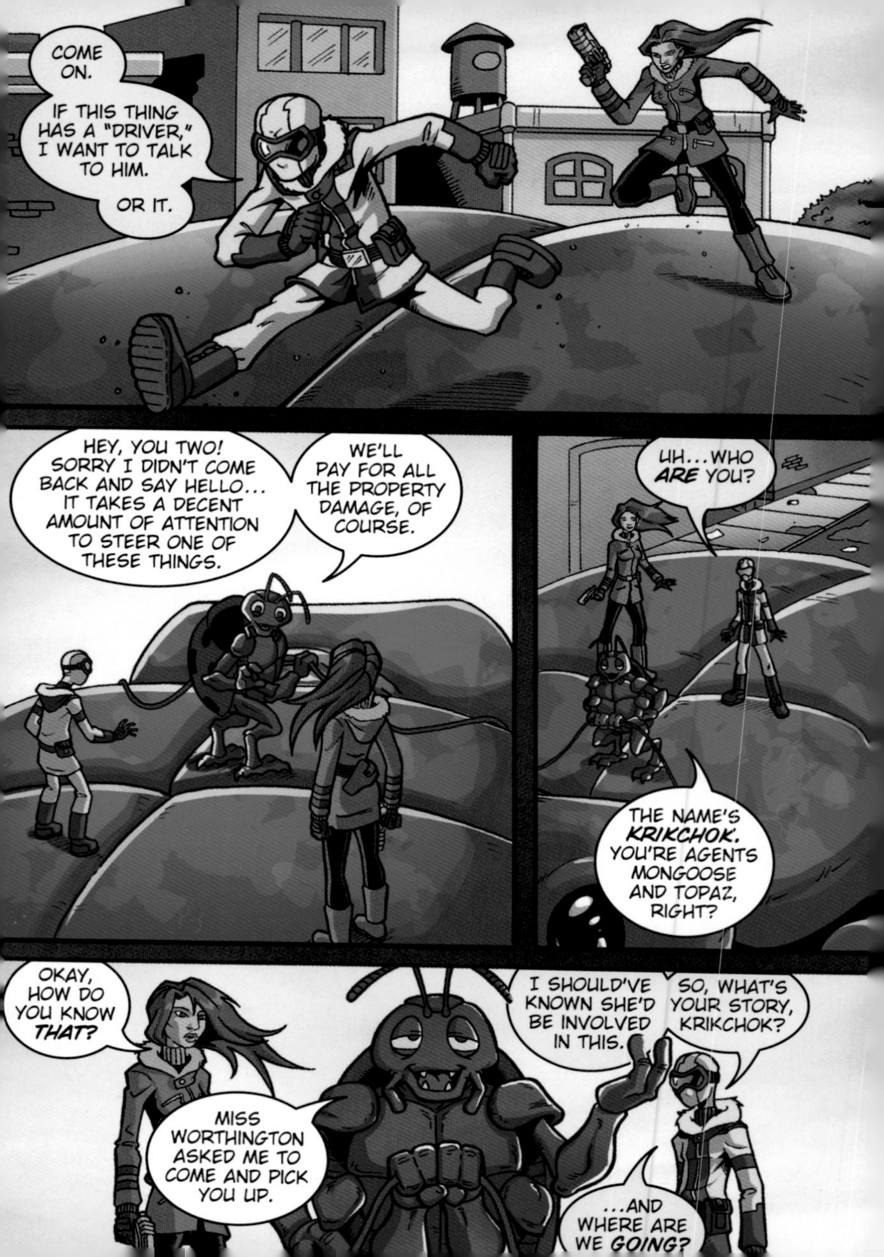
COME ON.
IF THIS THING HAS A "DRIVER," I WANT TO TALK TO HIM.
OR IT.
HEY, YOU TWO! SORRY I DIDN'T COME BACK AND SAY HELLO... IT TAKES A DECENT AMOUNT OF ATTENTION TO STEER ONE OF THESE THINGS.
WE'LL PAY FOR ALL THE PROPERTY DAMAGE, OF COURSE.
UH...WHO *ARE* YOU?
THE NAME'S ***KRIKCHOK.*** YOU'RE AGENTS MONGOOSE AND TOPAZ, RIGHT?
OKAY, HOW DO YOU KNOW ***THAT?***
MISS WORTHINGTON ASKED ME TO COME AND PICK YOU UP.
I SHOULD'VE KNOWN SHE'D BE INVOLVED IN THIS.
SO, WHAT'S YOUR STORY, KRIKCHOK?
...AND WHERE ARE WE ***GOING?***

"My people are what you might call 'space explorers,'
Krikchok says. "Unfortunately, a number of our advance
scouts to your planet disappeared off our radar. Only by
coming here in waves large enough to perform a search
did we discover that our scouts had been captured . . .
experimented upon . . . *controlled*."

You and Topaz both groan. "General Razonoff," you
grumble.

Krikchok's eyes light up. "Yes, that's the name! That's
the human responsible for all this."

"So . . . Krikchok . . ."

"Yes, Agent
Mongoose?"

"You don't blame
all humanity for what
happened to your scouts?"

"Oh, of course not! Why,
right now we're on our
way to talk to a meeting of
your world's leaders. It was
hastily arranged, from what
I understand, but should be
very productive. Would you
two like to accompany me?
We're going to a place called
'Moscow.'"

You both shrug. "Why not?"

GO ON TO THE NEXT PAGE.

As it turns out, Krikchok's people actually unite the whole human race, as they listen to him and his fellow insects.

You don't realize it at first, but you and Topaz are a part of history because of this. Today is the first day of the Human/Insect Peace Accord and Cooperative.

It's not long before the insects—who call themselves "the Armored Ones"—set up permanent bases on Earth and begin to trade with people. Then they casually mention that an Armored One ship will be leaving to explore new parts of space soon.

Miss Worthington and Krikchok have become fast friends, and Krikchok is waiting with her in her office. "How'd you like to see the stars, kid?" Krikchok asks you.

"You're inviting me . . . to go on a *spaceship*? Are you *kidding* me? Sign me up!"

Miss Worthington grins a little. "Don't say I never gave you anything."

THE END

DEALING WITH
EXPLOSIVES TAKES
YEARS OF CAREFUL
TRAINING AND MORE
RESPONSIBILITY THAN
MOST PEOPLE CAN
HANDLE.

LUCKILY, YOU'VE
GOT BOTH AND
THEN SOME.

ONCE YOU GET THESE
CHARGES SET AND HIT
THE TRANSMITTER,
THESE BUGS ARE
HISTORY.

OF COURSE...

...YOU MIGHT NOT
GET THAT CHANCE.

The company plane descends from a sky the color of snow and touches down on what appears to be an abandoned airfield. You slept as much as you could during the flight. You're not exactly sure how many hours have passed. You just know that you're about to step out onto Russian soil.

The agency has provided you with the best in cold-weather gear. As the plane's door opens and the exit ladder descends, you pull the hood of your parka closer around your face and emerge into glaring white sunlight.

Everything here seems to be white. The buildings are painted white. The ground is white with frost. And there are no people in sight anywhere.

Just as you begin to wonder if you're in the right place, a hatch opens in what you thought was solid, ice-covered ground. A hooded figure emerges and gives you a long look.

GO ON TO THE NEXT PAGE.

YOU'VE LEARNED TO MAKE **ABSOLUTELY** SURE YOU'RE DEALING WITH A REAL AGENT.

EXCHANGE OF **CODE PHRASES** COMES BEFORE **ANYTHING** ELSE.

"THE RAVEN FOLLOWS THE HAWK."

"TO THE OTHER SIDE OF THE RIDGE."

AGENT TOPAZ! AT LAST WE MEET IN PERSON.

AGENT **MONGOOSE.** YOUR REPUTATION PRECEDES YOU.

I THOUGHT YOU'D BE... TALLER. AND **OLDER.**

I GET THAT A LOT.

SHALL WE GET DOWN TO BUSINESS?

LEAD THE WAY.

TO BRING YOU UP TO SPEED: WE'VE MANAGED TO **CAPTURE** A **SPECIMEN.**

DO YOU WANT TO **SEE** IT, IN THE LAB?

OR DEPLOY DIRECTLY TO THE LAST REPORTED SIGHTING IN THE FIELD?

GO ON TO THE NEXT PAGE.

You normally want to get to the action as fast as possible. Of course, learning more about these creatures couldn't hurt, either.

WILL YOU . . .

. . . gather intel about this "specimen" they say they have?
TURN TO PAGE 89.

. . . forget about captive creatures and go after the ones on the loose?
TURN TO PAGE 106.

You take a deep breath and shout, "Look out, Topaz!" At the same instant, you jab the button on the transmitter, arming all the bombs.

Topaz whirls around, and you watch her throw a *beautiful* high roundhouse kick to the side of the mantis's head. It staggers and falls . . .

. . . but you have other problems to worry about. The bugs might not have noticed you when you were creeping around, but your shout has definitely got their attention now. You sprint toward Topaz and the tunnel to safety as dozens of enormous mantises swipe at you with their claws . . .

. . . and then you and Topaz are knocked flat by the bombs' detonation. The chamber with all the mantises inside has collapsed into a rocky heap.

Topaz sighs. "It'll cost a fortune to dig all that evidence out of there. Should've thought that through better."

You chuckle. "As long as they bill *you* and not *me*. It was your idea, y'know."

Topaz punches you in the shoulder with a laugh. Then you head back out together.

THE END

"Giant ants are dangerous, yes . . . but we have to neutralize the threat that wasp poses," you tell the scientists. Highbrow nods enthusiastically. He doesn't seem so scared now.

"What's got you worked up?" you ask him.

"Wasps are so *cool!*" he says. "They're not like bees—their stingers are smooth, so they can sting over and over! Each sting doesn't have as much venom as a bee's, but it really adds up fast!"

You frown at him. "What, and you think it's *neat* that one of those things is as big as you are now?"

Highbrow considers that, and his shoulders slump. He kicks the floor self-consciously. "Not *that* cool, I guess."

The lead scientist breaks in. "Look, we only bred the one wasp, but . . . it may have laid eggs. We've got to track this thing down before the eggs hatch, and destroy it and the eggs both."

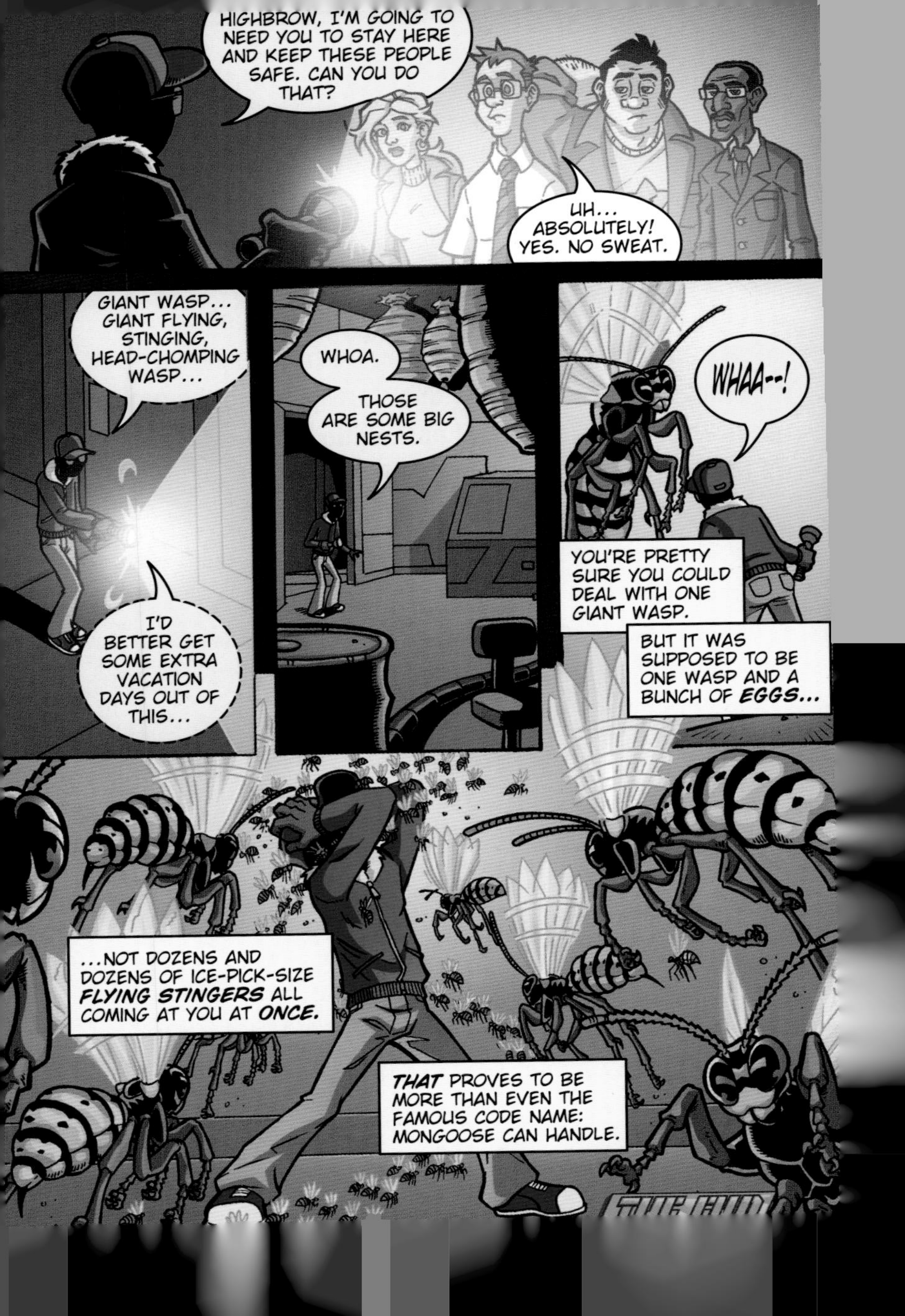
HIGHBROW, I'M GOING TO NEED YOU TO STAY HERE AND KEEP THESE PEOPLE SAFE. CAN YOU DO THAT?
UH... ABSOLUTELY! YES. NO SWEAT.
GIANT WASP... GIANT FLYING, STINGING, HEAD-CHOMPING WASP...
I'D BETTER GET SOME EXTRA VACATION DAYS OUT OF THIS...
WHOA.
THOSE ARE SOME BIG NESTS.
WHAA--!
YOU'RE PRETTY SURE YOU COULD DEAL WITH ONE GIANT WASP.
BUT IT WAS SUPPOSED TO BE ONE WASP AND A BUNCH OF EGGS...
...NOT DOZENS AND DOZENS OF ICE-PICK-SIZE FLYING STINGERS ALL COMING AT YOU AT ONCE.
THAT PROVES TO BE MORE THAN EVEN THE FAMOUS CODE NAME: MONGOOSE CAN HANDLE.

"I think this is the *perfect* time for a bath," Highbrow says, splashing into the rainwater puddle. "I can't think straight with my eyes watering and my nose hairs burning!" He notices you're not immediately following him and adds, "Believe me, you don't smell like a bed of roses yourself."

It *would* be nice not to have to breathe through your mouth anymore. You follow Highbrow into the puddle—it comes up to your ankles—and start splashing the cool, clean water over yourself. Almost immediately the stench of the ant scent grows less noticeable.

"Happy now?" you ask Highbrow.

"Ecstatic!"

"Good. Now let's figure out where this other agent is and how to find him."

But before you can get started, you hear the skittering sound of approaching ants.

Lots of them.

Lots and *lots* of them.

And you realize: without the pheromone scent on you . . . the ants recognize *you* as *food*.

THE END

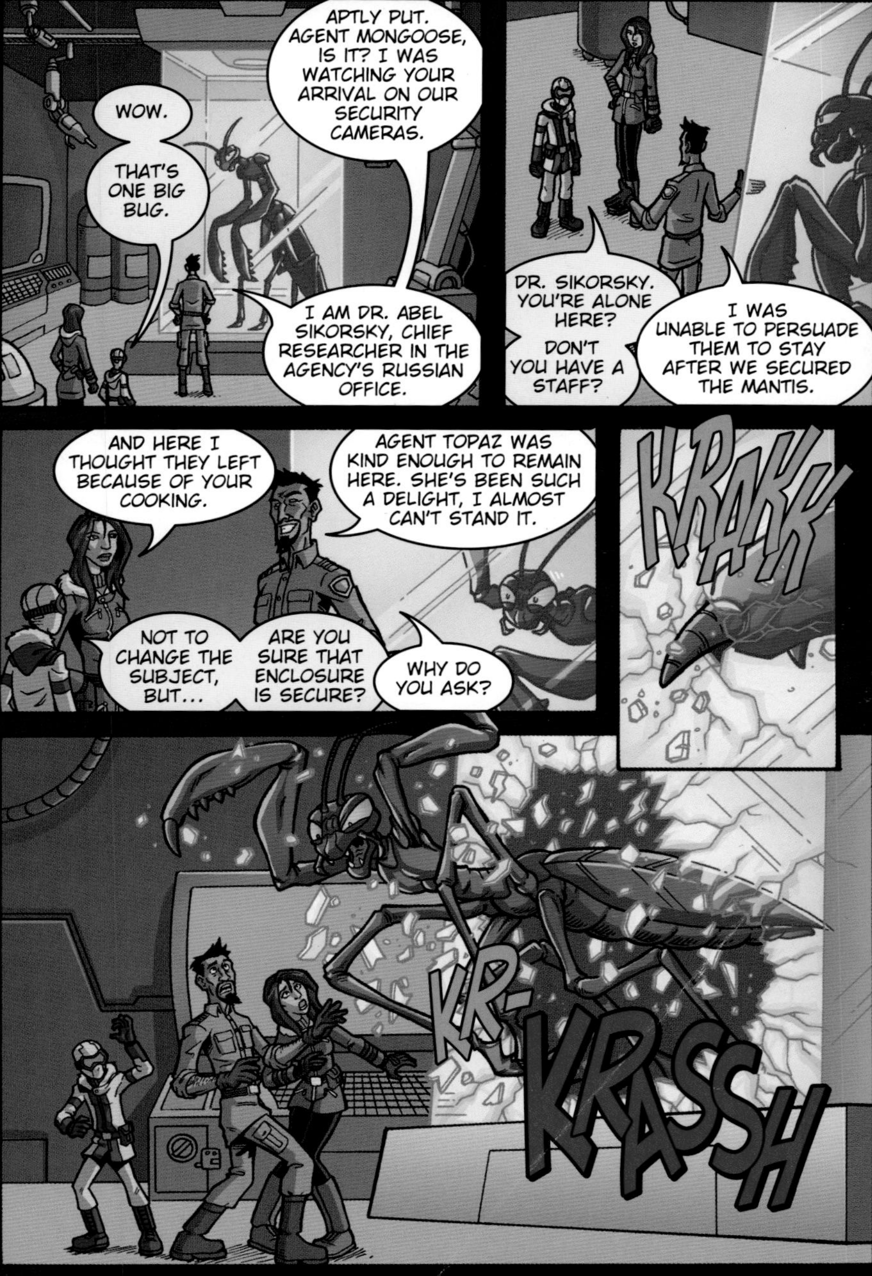
WOW.
THAT'S ONE BIG BUG.
APTLY PUT. AGENT MONGOOSE, IS IT? I WAS WATCHING YOUR ARRIVAL ON OUR SECURITY CAMERAS.
I AM DR. ABEL SIKORSKY, CHIEF RESEARCHER IN THE AGENCY'S RUSSIAN OFFICE.
DR. SIKORSKY. YOU'RE ALONE HERE?
DON'T YOU HAVE A STAFF?
I WAS UNABLE TO PERSUADE THEM TO STAY AFTER WE SECURED THE MANTIS.
AND HERE I THOUGHT THEY LEFT BECAUSE OF YOUR COOKING.
AGENT TOPAZ WAS KIND ENOUGH TO REMAIN HERE. SHE'S BEEN SUCH A DELIGHT, I ALMOST CAN'T STAND IT.
NOT TO CHANGE THE SUBJECT, BUT...
ARE YOU SURE THAT ENCLOSURE IS SECURE?
WHY DO YOU ASK?
KRAKK
KR-KRASSH

GO ON TO THE NEXT PAGE.

With that monstrosity on the loose, you know you've got to do something *immediately*.

WILL YOU . . .

. . . stay here and try to incapacitate the mantis?
TURN TO PAGE 48.

. . . take Topaz and Sikorsky and try to seal off the lab?
TURN TO PAGE 32.

Topaz fires her SINDR, and the mantis falls to the ground, unconscious.

And behind you, someone claps. "Well done," General Razonoff says as you spin around. Topaz tries to shoot the general, but suddenly he *blurs* with speed. Razonoff rips the gun out of her hand, spins, and punches you square in the jaw.

"What's going on?" you mutter, trying to get up off the floor.

"I'll show you," Razonoff says—and his skin splits open. A huge, grotesque alien insect steps out of the General Razonoff suit and clacks its mandibles at you. "All these insects are *my* servants . . . my army. Except for the stupid mantises. They were trying to stop me."

He grabs Topaz's chin with one claw. "But you two made sure that one didn't get in the way, didn't you? I appreciate that."

It sinks in at that moment: the "general" won't be letting you leave.

Ever.

THE END

You've got to detonate these bombs—but you've got to help Topaz too!

WILL YOU . . .

. . . set off the bombs and then try to get Topaz out of trouble?

TURN TO PAGE 85.

. . . forget about the bombs for now and help Topaz as quickly as possible?

TURN TO PAGE 30.

You look at Topaz, your forehead wrinkling. "Listen, if we destroy that portal without understanding what it is or where it leads, we could be losing critical information. Information Miss Worthington would *really* want to have."

Topaz sighs, reluctant. "We could also be passing up the opportunity to shut down the source of all these monster bugs."

"Right, but what if it turns out they're from some world that could really help us out? Or some world that *we* could really help out? What if these bugs are, like, the worst thing that ever happened to some other planet, and they never figured out how to make bug spray? If we don't investigate, we could be dooming someone else to a horrible giant bug fate!"

"Good grief," Topaz says, "I don't know whether to laugh or cheer. Fine, we'll do it your way. I just hope this doesn't come back to haunt us."

GO ON TO THE NEXT PAGE.

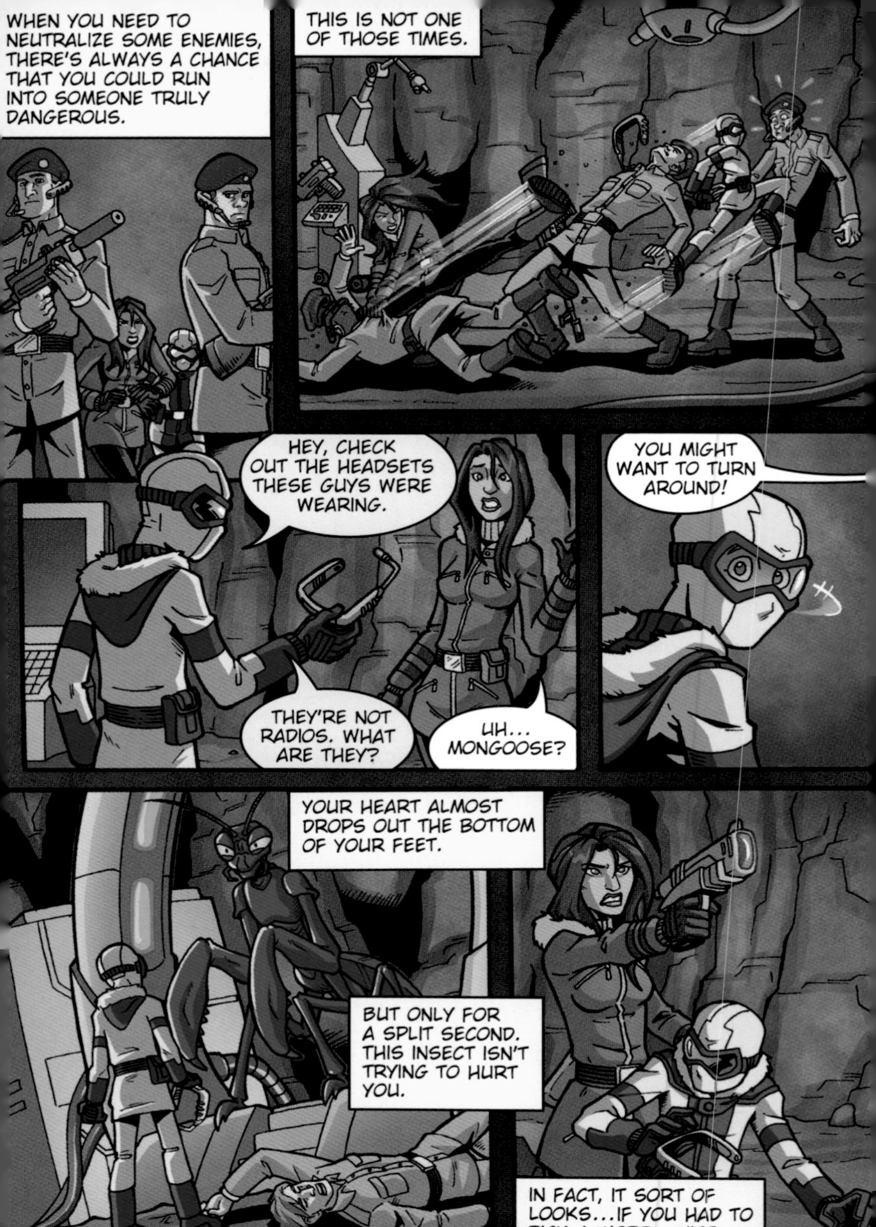
WHEN YOU NEED TO NEUTRALIZE SOME ENEMIES, THERE'S ALWAYS A CHANCE THAT YOU COULD RUN INTO SOMEONE TRULY DANGEROUS.
THIS IS NOT ONE OF THOSE TIMES.
HEY, CHECK OUT THE HEADSETS THESE GUYS WERE WEARING.
THEY'RE NOT RADIOS. WHAT ARE THEY?
UH... MONGOOSE?
YOU MIGHT WANT TO TURN AROUND!
YOUR HEART ALMOST DROPS OUT THE BOTTOM OF YOUR FEET.
BUT ONLY FOR A SPLIT SECOND. THIS INSECT ISN'T TRYING TO HURT YOU.
IN FACT, IT SORT OF LOOKS...IF YOU HAD TO PICK A WORD...NICE.

You and Topaz exchange glances. She gives you a tiny, subtle nod . . . and the two of you launch yourselves at the half-bug creature.

It leaps backward, at least 15 feet in the air, and lands, scowling. "What do you hope to accomplish with this? We've won! We've taken over your country—your whole planet! You two aren't even considered a threat! That's why I'm the only one talking to you!"

"Then stop talking," you bark and shoot the creature with your SINDR. It falls to the ground, unconscious.

"You think it was telling the truth?" Topaz asks. "Think the whole world belongs to them now?"

"Maybe," you reply. "But if that's the case, we've got our work cut out for us."

"How so?"

"Simple. There have to be other humans still out there somewhere. We're going to find them. And then we'll take the world back."

She grins. "Let's go!"

THE END

You wriggle back toward Topaz just as silently as you came. She's waiting in a darkened corner and listens quietly as you explain to her what you saw in the general's war room.

"If we take out Razonoff, the rest of these guys should be much easier to get rid of," you say, excited.

"Yeah, that'd be great," she agrees, "but there's a problem. Could you see the *entire* room from where you were?"

"Well . . . uh . . . no."

"So there could be too many guards in there for us to deal with."

You shrug. "Okay. What do *you* think we should do?"

"I think we've got two choices. One, you and I go back through the vent and try to handle whatever's in the room. Two, we create a series of distractions that draw all the guards away from the eggs *and* Razonoff. Then we go get him. I like the second choice."

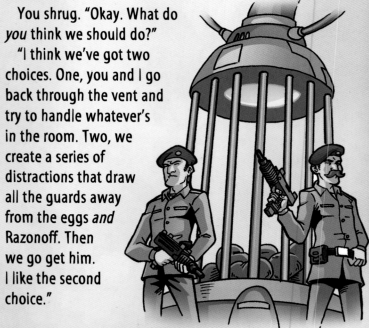

You can see the merit in both options.

WILL YOU . . .

. . . try to distract the guards?
TURN TO PAGE 50.

. . . go for broke and try to take out
General Razonoff first thing?
TURN TO PAGE 8.

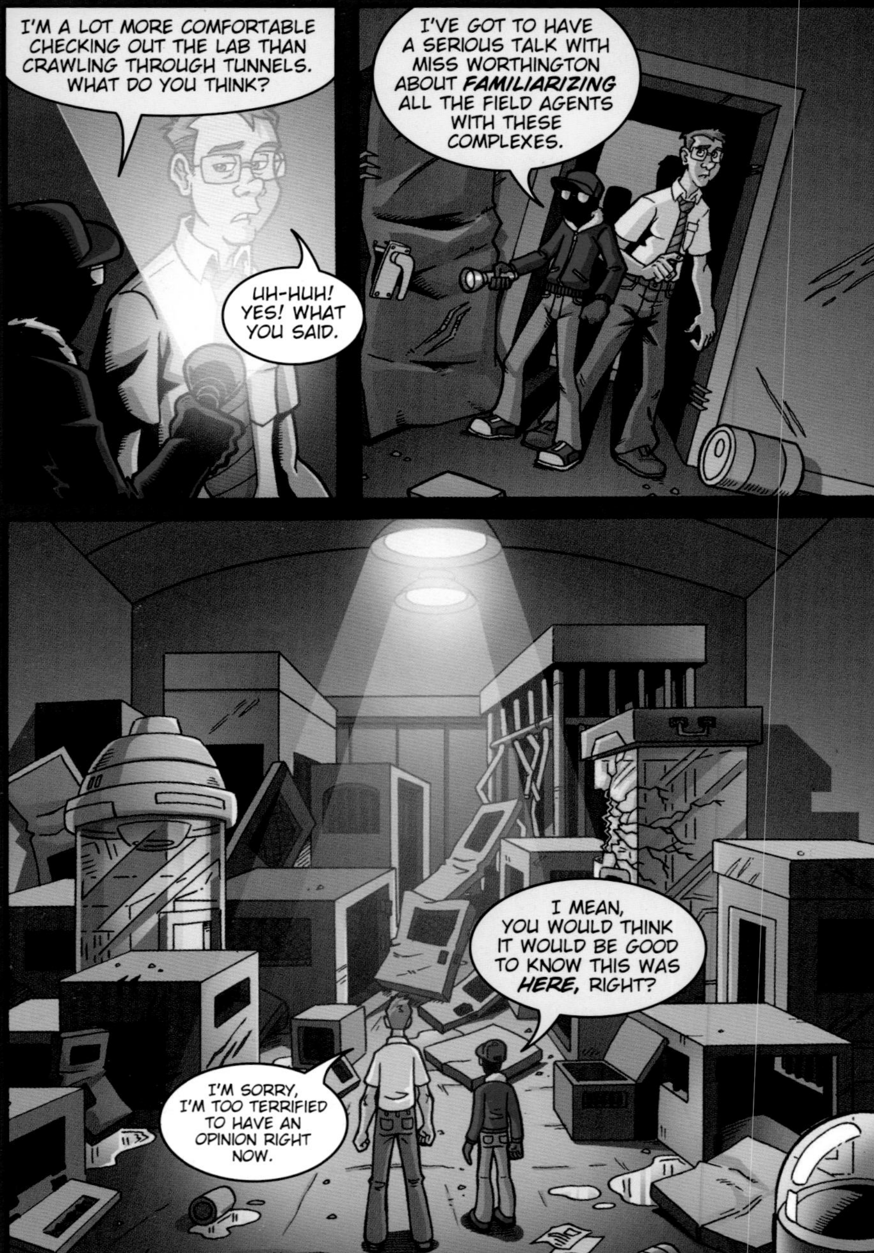

I'M A LOT MORE COMFORTABLE CHECKING OUT THE LAB THAN CRAWLING THROUGH TUNNELS. WHAT DO YOU THINK?
UH-HUH! YES! WHAT YOU SAID.
I'VE GOT TO HAVE A SERIOUS TALK WITH MISS WORTHINGTON ABOUT ***FAMILIARIZING*** ALL THE FIELD AGENTS WITH THESE COMPLEXES.
I MEAN, YOU WOULD THINK IT WOULD BE GOOD TO KNOW THIS WAS ***HERE,*** RIGHT?
I'M SORRY, I'M TOO TERRIFIED TO HAVE AN OPINION RIGHT NOW.

GO ON TO THE NEXT PAGE.

You take a long look at the various enclosures and cages in this lab. Something's wrong here. Something's *very* wrong here.

Moving down a row of cages, you find a sight you never expected to see: the cast-off shell of a cicada—*as big as a Great Dane*. Pellets the size of your fist litter the floor of the cage . . . and everything becomes crystal clear in a flash.

"These bugs—they didn't tunnel their way in here from outside. They were *grown* here! *We* grew them!"

Highbrow slowly raises his palms in a sort of helpless gesture. "Uh . . . oops?"

Frowning, you point at a big set of double doors at the far end of the lab. "Come on. We've got to find out if there's anybody else stuck down here. I *particularly* want to talk to whoever's in charge of this little 'experiment.'"

GO ON TO THE NEXT PAGE.

Through the double doors is another lab—and at the far end of it, behind a hastily built barricade, you discover a group of scientists, quaking in fear. One of them squeals, "Don't hurt us! Don't hurt us!"

"Relax," you tell him, as the three researchers shakily stand up. "Who are you? What is this place?"

"W-we were trying to breed super-large insects for the m-military," the lead scientist says.

"All right. What *exactly* are we dealing with then?"

"We bred giant ants, giant ant lions, praying mantises, and, uh, one really big wasp. The ant lions haven't gotten out yet. They're in a holding room behind us. They, uh . . . they *eat* ants, you see. The ants are out there—they chased us in here!"

"And where is this wasp?" you demand.

"I don't know. All I can tell you is that it's insanely dangerous."

Ants . . . ant lions . . . wasps . . .

Hmmm.

100

GO ON TO THE NEXT PAGE.

TWISTED JOURNEYS®

You've never tried to subdue a giant wasp on your own before . . . but then again, you've never intentionally released a bunch of weird mutant ant-eating bugs, either.

WILL YOU . . .

. . . try to take on the wasp yourself?
TURN TO PAGE 86.

. . . put your faith in the scientists and release the ant lions?
TURN TO PAGE 22.

THIS CREATURE MAY *BE* SMART.

BUT THE QUESTION IS: IS IT SMARTER THAN *YOU* ARE?

AND AS IT TAKES THE BAIT YOU SET UP...

...YOU'RE PRETTY SURE THE ANSWER IS NO.

AFTER DEALING WITH THE WASP, TAKING CARE OF A FEW *ANTS* SHOULD BE A PIECE OF CAKE.

THE END

102

"I guess you're right," Highbrow admits. "If that signal is strong enough, we should keep following it."

You lead the way, moving farther and farther into the colony. The ants don't bother you, and you realize it must be because of the "ant juice"—these insects think you're ants too!

The distress signal changes from a beeping to a steady buzz. "It's just ahead," you whisper to Highbrow, and you step through . . .

. . . into the queen's chamber! A massive ant, easily the size of a car, rests in the center of this place, surrounded by hundreds of eggs. And there on the floor is the distress beacon you've been picking up. "One of the ants must have carried this down here," you whisper to Highbrow.

Quietly the two of you retreat. You'll be able to return with all the backup you need to deal with the ants.

Thank goodness for ant juice!

THE END

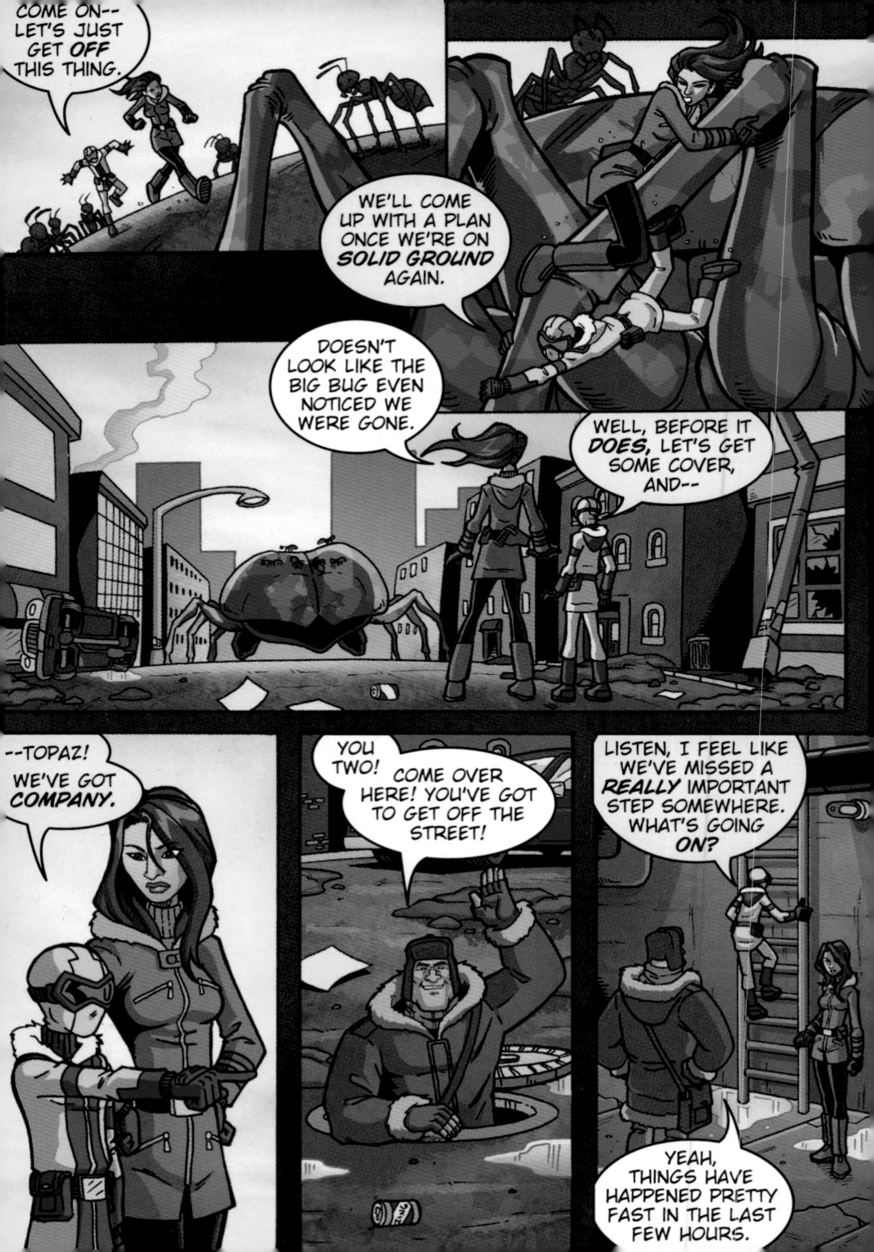
COME ON-- LET'S JUST GET **OFF** THIS THING.
WE'LL COME UP WITH A PLAN ONCE WE'RE ON **SOLID GROUND** AGAIN.
DOESN'T LOOK LIKE THE BIG BUG EVEN NOTICED WE WERE GONE.
WELL, BEFORE IT **DOES,** LET'S GET SOME COVER, AND--
--TOPAZ! WE'VE GOT **COMPANY.**
YOU TWO!
COME OVER HERE! YOU'VE GOT TO GET OFF THE STREET!
LISTEN, I FEEL LIKE WE'VE MISSED A **REALLY** IMPORTANT STEP SOMEWHERE. WHAT'S GOING **ON?**
YEAH, THINGS HAVE HAPPENED PRETTY FAST IN THE LAST FEW HOURS.

Your guide tells you that the giant bugs are overrunning the planet. "They're everywhere," he says. A human resistance sprang up immediately, led by someone all the fighters refer to as Her Highness.

Soon you enter a big circular room with a makeshift table and some scrounged chairs in it. A few ragged but tough-looking people are perched in the chairs . . . and sitting at the table's head is someone with whom you are *very* familiar.

"I should've known," you say, smiling. "Your Highness, I presume?"

Miss Worthington stands up from the table. "Mongoose. Topaz. Good to see you. Now, fall in. I need to brief you."

"On what?" Topaz asks.

"Just because huge bugs have *taken* the world, doesn't mean we're going to let them *keep* it. We are the resistance now. So listen up! I've got your first assignment."

You know the old saying. The more things change . . .

THE END

You and Topaz take one of the agency's helicopters. She fills you in on your destination while you're in the air.

"We're headed to Rasputinov Prison," she tells you through your radio earphones. "It's been abandoned for the last 40 years, but the government still performs a little bit of upkeep. Some of the workers swear they saw a giant praying mantis there."

"Well, let's check it out then."

The two of you land in the middle of a huge prison complex with a beautiful cathedral in its center. You decide to start with the cathedral and work your way out from there . . .

. . . but you're not in the building more than a minute before you spot some strange scratch marks near one of the floor tiles.

"Help me with this, would you?" you ask.

Topaz comes over, and the two of you lift the tile— revealing a secret passageway.

GO ON TO THE NEXT PAGE.

THIS IS PRE-SOVIET CONSTRUCTION, SO WATCH YOUR HEAD. SOME OF IT HOLDS UP, AND SOME OF IT DOESN'T.

WE *WOULD* HAVE USED RADAR TO TRY TO PINPOINT ANY UNUSUAL ACTIVITY HERE, BUT THE BUILDING'S CONSTRUCTION HAS MADE THAT IMPOSSIBLE.

I'VE ALWAYS PREFERRED A MORE HANDS-ON APPROACH MYSELF.

WOULDN'T WANT YOU TO GET A CHUNK OF ROCK THROUGH YOUR SKULL.

THAT'S VERY CONSIDERATE OF YOU.

WELL, HERE'S YOUR CHANCE.

THIS PRISON MAY NOT BE IN USE, BUT IT'S *DEFINITELY* NOT ABANDONED.

FROM ONE PASSAGEWAY AHEAD, YOU CAN HEAR HUMAN VOICES.

FROM ANOTHER, A KIND OF *SKITTERING* SOUND THAT MAKES THE HAIRS ON THE BACK OF YOUR NECK STAND UP.

AND FROM THE THIRD, A STRANGE GLOW EMANATES.

GO ON TO THE NEXT PAGE.

You know the giant bugs really exist now . . . but could there be *humans* behind this whole thing?

WILL YOU . . .

. . . identify whatever's making those sounds, so you'll know what you're up against?

TURN TO PAGE 63.

. . . get to the source of the voices?

TURN TO PAGE 39.

. . . put sounds and voices on hold and see what's causing that weird glow?

TURN TO PAGE 31.

You figure you'd better keep this flying monster right where you can see it—and that means fighting it, right there in the lab.

It lunges at you, driving that huge stinger forward, but you slip out of the way. The stinger clangs off a metal shelf, knocking the whole shelf unit down . . .

. . . and you see a crack in the wall where the shelves used to be. A crack just about the right size . . . !

You duck the stinger two more times and scramble over to the wall, climbing on the fallen shelves. The wasp comes in for one more attack—and as you twist to the side, the stinger jams into the crack and gets caught!

You grab the wasp and shove the stinger farther in, trapping it.

The wasp whines at you, furious but helpless.

With the wasp neutralized . . . and the scientists safe . . . now you can concentrate on getting some reinforcements down here!

THE END

The bizarre half-human, half-insect creature grins. Then it laughs comfortingly and claps its bizarre hands on both your shoulders and Topaz's, hard enough to sting.

"Relax, relax, you're both fine! We're all friends here, aren't we?"

"But . . ." Topaz tries to step away. "What's happened here? What happened to the White House? What happened to the *world*?"

The half bug frowns. "Well, if I had to guess, I'd say you two got punted through time a little bit."

"What?" You can't believe it. *"Time travel?"*

"Only a little bit," the half bug says. "Just far enough to see the result of our invasion. It's an insect nation now, my mammalian friends! And . . . you two want to swear allegiance to it, don't you?"

It's then that you realize—the bug must have injected you both with some sort of mind-altering venom!

Because you hear yourself say, "Yes . . . yes . . . tell me more, master . . ."

THE END

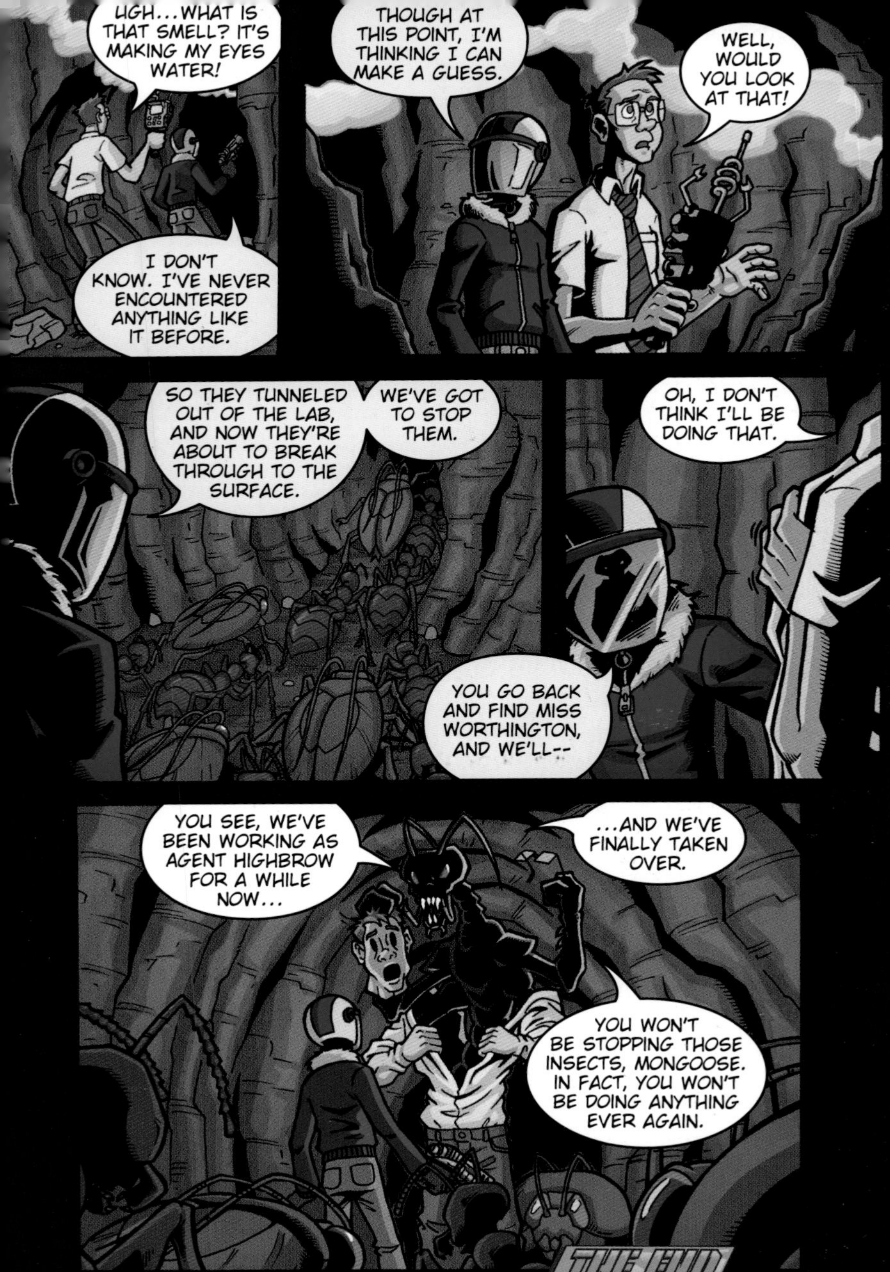
UGH...WHAT IS THAT SMELL? IT'S MAKING MY EYES WATER!
I DON'T KNOW. I'VE NEVER ENCOUNTERED ANYTHING LIKE IT BEFORE.
THOUGH AT THIS POINT, I'M THINKING I CAN MAKE A GUESS.
WELL, WOULD YOU LOOK AT THAT!
SO THEY TUNNELED OUT OF THE LAB, AND NOW THEY'RE ABOUT TO BREAK THROUGH TO THE SURFACE.
WE'VE GOT TO STOP THEM.
YOU GO BACK AND FIND MISS WORTHINGTON, AND WE'LL--
OH, I DON'T THINK I'LL BE DOING THAT.
YOU SEE, WE'VE BEEN WORKING AS AGENT HIGHBROW FOR A WHILE NOW...
...AND WE'VE FINALLY TAKEN OVER.
YOU WON'T BE STOPPING THOSE INSECTS, MONGOOSE. IN FACT, YOU WON'T BE DOING ANYTHING EVER AGAIN.
THE END

EXPERIENCE ALL OF THE

TWISTED JOURNEYS®

#1 CAPTURED BY PIRATES
Will these scurvy pirates turn you into shark bait?

#2 ESCAPE FROM PYRAMID X
Not every ancient mummy stays dead . . .

#3 TERROR IN GHOST MANSION
The spooks in this Halloween house aren't wearing costumes . . .

#4 THE TREASURE OF MOUNT FATE
Can you survive monsters and magic and bring home the treasure?

#5 NIGHTM
Will you be th

#6 THE TIM
Danger is ever
in a time mac

#7 VAMPIRE
These vampire

#8 ALIEN IN
Make peace w
never get off their planet . . .

#9 AGENT MONGOOSE AND THE HYPNO-BEAM SCHEME
Your top-secret mission: foil the plots of an evil mastermind!

#10 THE GOBLIN KING
Will you join the fearsome goblins or the dangerous elves?

#11 SHIPWRECKED ON MAD ISLAND
Mad scientists and mutants are on your trail!

#12 KUNG FU MASTERS
Can you master kung fu in time to battle bandits and ghosts?

#13 SCHOOL OF EVIL
The teachers are creepy, monsters lurk in the lab, and your dorm room is haunted!

#14 ATTACK OF THE MUTANT METEORS
Can you survive being sky-tall or bug-small?

#15 AGENT MONGOOSE AND THE ATTACK OF THE GIANT INSECTS
Your top-secret mission: squash a bug invasion!

#16 THE QUEST FOR DRAGON MOUNTAIN
Will you hoard gold or seek adventure? You're the dragon, you decide!

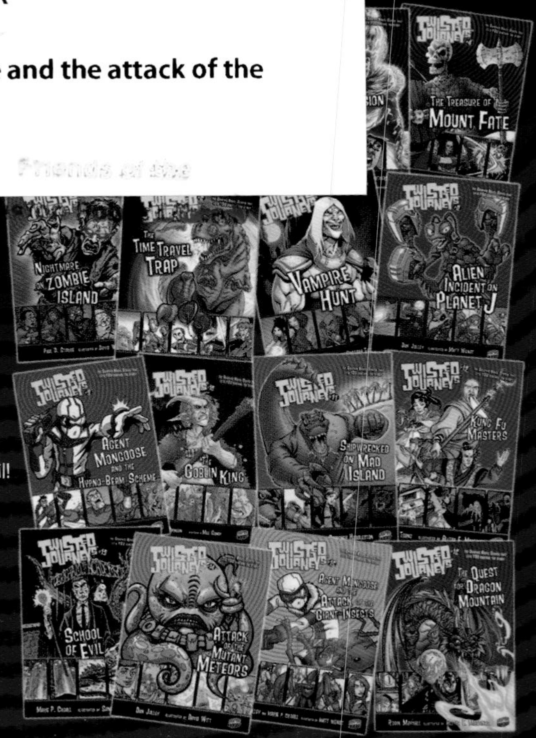
The Treasure of Mount Fate
Nightmare on Zombie Island
The Time Travel Trap
Vampire Hunt
Alien Incident on Planet J
Agent Mongoose and the Hypno-Beam Scheme
The Goblin King
Shipwrecked on Mad Island
Kung Fu Masters
School of Evil
Attack of the Mutant Meteors
Agent Mongoose and the Attack of the Giant Insects
The Quest for Dragon Mountain